ALREADY

LURED

(A Laura Frost Suspense Thriller—Book Ten)

BLAKE PIERCE

Blake Pierce

Blake Pierce is the USA Today bestselling author of the RILEY PAGE mystery series, which includes seventeen books. Blake Pierce is also the author of the MACKENZIE WHITE mystery series, comprising fourteen books; of the AVERY BLACK mystery series, comprising six books; of the KERI LOCKE mystery series, comprising five books; of the MAKING OF RILEY PAIGE mystery series, comprising six books; of the KATE WISE mystery series, comprising seven books; of the CHLOE FINE psychological suspense mystery, comprising six books; of the JESSIE HUNT psychological suspense thriller series, comprising twenty six books; of the AU PAIR psychological suspense thriller series, comprising three books; of the ZOE PRIME mystery series, comprising six books; of the ADELE SHARP mystery series, comprising sixteen books, of the EUROPEAN VOYAGE cozy mystery series, comprising six books; of the LAURA FROST FBI suspense thriller, comprising eleven books; of the ELLA DARK FBI suspense thriller, comprising fourteen books (and counting); of the A YEAR IN EUROPE cozy mystery series, comprising nine books, of the AVA GOLD mystery series, comprising six books; of the RACHEL GIFT mystery series, comprising ten books (and counting); of the VALERIE LAW mystery series, comprising nine books (and counting); of the PAIGE KING mystery series, comprising eight books (and counting); of the MAY MOORE mystery series, comprising eleven books (and counting); the CORA SHIELDS mystery series, comprising five books (and counting); of the NICKY LYONS mystery series, comprising seven books (and counting), of the CAMI LARK mystery series, comprising five books (and counting), and of the new AMBER YOUNG mystery series, comprising five books (and counting).

An avid reader and lifelong fan of the mystery and thriller genres, Blake loves to hear from you, so please feel free to visit www.blakepierceauthor.com to learn more and stay in touch.

ISBN: 978-1-0943-8047-6

BOOKS BY BLAKE PIERCE

AMBER YOUNG MYSTERY SERIES
ABSENT PITY (Book #1)
ABSENT REMORSE (Book #2)
ABSENT FEELING (Book #3)
ABSENT MERCY (Book #4)
ABSENT REASON (Book #5)

CAMI LARK MYSTERY SERIES
JUST ME (Book #1)
JUST OUTSIDE (Book #2)
JUST RIGHT (Book #3)
JUST FORGET (Book #4)
JUST ONCE (Book #5)

NICKY LYONS MYSTERY SERIES
ALL MINE (Book #1)
ALL HIS (Book #2)
ALL HE SEES (Book #3)
ALL ALONE (Book #4)
ALL FOR ONE (Book #5)
ALL HE TAKES (Book #6)
ALL FOR ME (Book #7)

CORA SHIELDS MYSTERY SERIES
UNDONE (Book #1)
UNWANTED (Book #2)
UNHINGED (Book #3)
UNSAID (Book #4)
UNGLUED (Book #5)

MAY MOORE SUSPENSE THRILLER
NEVER RUN (Book #1)
NEVER TELL (Book #2)
NEVER LIVE (Book #3)
NEVER HIDE (Book #4)
NEVER FORGIVE (Book #5)

NEVER AGAIN (Book #6)
NEVER LOOK BACK (Book #7)
NEVER FORGET (Book #8)
NEVER LET GO (Book #9)
NEVER PRETEND (Book #10)
NEVER HESITATE (Book #11)

PAIGE KING MYSTERY SERIES
THE GIRL HE PINED (Book #1)
THE GIRL HE CHOSE (Book #2)
THE GIRL HE TOOK (Book #3)
THE GIRL HE WISHED (Book #4)
THE GIRL HE CROWNED (Book #5)
THE GIRL HE WATCHED (Book #6)
THE GIRL HE WANTED (Book #7)
THE GIRL HE CLAIMED (Book #8)

VALERIE LAW MYSTERY SERIES
NO MERCY (Book #1)
NO PITY (Book #2)
NO FEAR (Book #3)
NO SLEEP (Book #4)
NO QUARTER (Book #5)
NO CHANCE (Book #6)
NO REFUGE (Book #7)
NO GRACE (Book #8)
NO ESCAPE (Book #9)

RACHEL GIFT MYSTERY SERIES
HER LAST WISH (Book #1)
HER LAST CHANCE (Book #2)
HER LAST HOPE (Book #3)
HER LAST FEAR (Book #4)
HER LAST CHOICE (Book #5)
HER LAST BREATH (Book #6)
HER LAST MISTAKE (Book #7)
HER LAST DESIRE (Book #8)
HER LAST REGRET (Book #9)
HER LAST HOUR (Book #10)

AVA GOLD MYSTERY SERIES

CITY OF PREY (Book #1)
CITY OF FEAR (Book #2)
CITY OF BONES (Book #3)
CITY OF GHOSTS (Book #4)
CITY OF DEATH (Book #5)
CITY OF VICE (Book #6)

A YEAR IN EUROPE
A MURDER IN PARIS (Book #1)
DEATH IN FLORENCE (Book #2)
VENGEANCE IN VIENNA (Book #3)
A FATALITY IN SPAIN (Book #4)

ELLA DARK FBI SUSPENSE THRILLER
GIRL, ALONE (Book #1)
GIRL, TAKEN (Book #2)
GIRL, HUNTED (Book #3)
GIRL, SILENCED (Book #4)
GIRL, VANISHED (Book 5)
GIRL ERASED (Book #6)
GIRL, FORSAKEN (Book #7)
GIRL, TRAPPED (Book #8)
GIRL, EXPENDABLE (Book #9)
GIRL, ESCAPED (Book #10)
GIRL, HIS (Book #11)
GIRL, LURED (Book #12)
GIRL, MISSING (Book #13)
GIRL, UNKNOWN (Book #14)

LAURA FROST FBI SUSPENSE THRILLER
ALREADY GONE (Book #1)
ALREADY SEEN (Book #2)
ALREADY TRAPPED (Book #3)
ALREADY MISSING (Book #4)
ALREADY DEAD (Book #5)
ALREADY TAKEN (Book #6)
ALREADY CHOSEN (Book #7)
ALREADY LOST (Book #8)
ALREADY HIS (Book #9)
ALREADY LURED (Book #10)
ALREADY COLD (Book #11)

CHLOE FINE PSYCHOLOGICAL SUSPENSE SERIES

KATE WISE MYSTERY SERIES

IF SHE FEARED (Book #6)
IF SHE HEARD (Book #7)

THE MAKING OF RILEY PAIGE SERIES
WATCHING (Book #1)
WAITING (Book #2)
LURING (Book #3)
TAKING (Book #4)
STALKING (Book #5)
KILLING (Book #6)

RILEY PAIGE MYSTERY SERIES
ONCE GONE (Book #1)
ONCE TAKEN (Book #2)
ONCE CRAVED (Book #3)
ONCE LURED (Book #4)
ONCE HUNTED (Book #5)
ONCE PINED (Book #6)
ONCE FORSAKEN (Book #7)
ONCE COLD (Book #8)
ONCE STALKED (Book #9)
ONCE LOST (Book #10)
ONCE BURIED (Book #11)
ONCE BOUND (Book #12)
ONCE TRAPPED (Book #13)
ONCE DORMANT (Book #14)
ONCE SHUNNED (Book #15)
ONCE MISSED (Book #16)
ONCE CHOSEN (Book #17)

MACKENZIE WHITE MYSTERY SERIES
BEFORE HE KILLS (Book #1)
BEFORE HE SEES (Book #2)
BEFORE HE COVETS (Book #3)
BEFORE HE TAKES (Book #4)
BEFORE HE NEEDS (Book #5)
BEFORE HE FEELS (Book #6)
BEFORE HE SINS (Book #7)
BEFORE HE HUNTS (Book #8)
BEFORE HE PREYS (Book #9)
BEFORE HE LONGS (Book #10)

BEFORE HE LAPSES (Book #11)
BEFORE HE ENVIES (Book #12)
BEFORE HE STALKS (Book #13)
BEFORE HE HARMS (Book #14)

AVERY BLACK MYSTERY SERIES
CAUSE TO KILL (Book #1)
CAUSE TO RUN (Book #2)
CAUSE TO HIDE (Book #3)
CAUSE TO FEAR (Book #4)
CAUSE TO SAVE (Book #5)
CAUSE TO DREAD (Book #6)

KERI LOCKE MYSTERY SERIES
A TRACE OF DEATH (Book #1)
A TRACE OF MURDER (Book #2)
A TRACE OF VICE (Book #3)
A TRACE OF CRIME (Book #4)
A TRACE OF HOPE (Book #5)

CHAPTER ONE

Jessika smiled, a reassuring and soft expression crossing over her face. A purposefully built expression, intended to do the very important work of putting her client at ease. He was very much in need of positive reinforcement whenever he achieved something, or he would end up going backwards in another few sessions. That was something she'd always noticed with him.

"Well done," she said warmly. "That was a big step forward. I'm very proud of the progress you've made this week."

"Thanks," he said, wiping away a tear around his eye and sniffling. "I do feel better."

"That's fantastic," Jessika told him. "Now we just have to keep that progress up. Okay?"

"Yeah," he sniffed, nodding. That was good enough for her.

"Alright, Brian," she said. "That's it for today. Well done, again. I'll see you at the same time next week."

Brian nodded, getting up. "Thanks," he said. "Um. Have a good week."

"You too, Brian," Jessika said, smiling warmly but then looking down at her notes and pretending to expand on them with her pen. She'd found it was the only reliable way to get Brian to leave. If she didn't make it clear she was disengaging from him, he would linger for as long as he could. He always wanted to prolong the conversation for as long as possible.

Unfortunately, she suspected that was why he had specifically requested the last slot of her working day. It meant he knew she was never in a rush to get to the next client, only to return home. He could always rely on being able to delay her because he knew full well there was no one else waiting.

Brian lingered awkwardly for a moment before taking the hint and slowly making his way to the door. Jessika felt his eyes on her, knew he was pausing there as he always did. If she looked up now, he would see it as an invitation to turn back and walk towards her again and then speak.

The door opened and closed, and Jessika felt her shoulders relaxing in relief.

She looked up to be certain, seeing that she was alone in her office at last. She sighed, putting a hand up to her shoulder to push and pull at the muscle there and try to ease the knots that had formed. She wouldn't change a thing about her job – she loved helping other people. But there were days when being a therapist felt harder for her than others. Days when she had to take the time to remember that she, too, was a human being, with the same emotions and needs that the rest of them had.

She closed her eyes and worked her thumb and forefinger over her forehead and temples, soothing away the headache that had been forming all day. Not long, she told herself, and she would be able to get home to a nice glass of wine, a pasta meal, and something mindless on the television before sleep.

First, she had to finish her debriefing for the day. There were patient notes to compile, notes to type, medication requests to review. As she did every day, she would finish off by looking at the next day's patients and considering them, so that she was in the right mental space when she approached her work in the morning.

Maybe it was just the fact that it was the first Friday after the Christmas and New Year's break that had her feeling the strain. It always seemed harder to get back to work after a break. And though she'd been able to spend the holidays with her parents, it was always just one more reminder that she didn't yet have the things they frequently expressed they wanted for her. The patter of the tiny feet of children filling the rooms of her home. A bigger practice, maybe in a bigger city. A more worthy partner, because they had never approved of Jessika's wife and made no secret of that fact.

In fact, Ginny was a saint for putting up with it over those few days they spent with her family. Just one more reason to remember that the life she had was good enough, thank you, and that she enjoyed it. Jessika told herself the mantra she frequently told her patients: focus on the things you do have, not the things you don't.

Jessika finished typing up her notes on Brian in her computer and saved the program, shutting everything down. Finally done with the day, she glanced over the schedule for tomorrow and then at the clock. It was getting late already. Why did the work always seem to take the longest when you were the most eager to get home?

She would think about the plan for tomorrow in the car. She scooped up her home and car keys from her desk drawer and headed over to the door, grabbing her coat from the rack as she passed it and shrugging it onto her shoulders. Her purse joined the coat and then she was on her way out, locking the door behind her and glancing around in the dark.

And it was dark out – stunningly dark. There were clouds over the moon, or maybe there was no moon at all tonight – she couldn't even tell. It was only a short walk from the office to the parking lot, which served not just her but a row of businesses on the outskirts of town, but it made her feel nervous every time. She looked forward to the summer months, when she would stride across this distance with confidence, her head high. Then she would worry more about her heels sinking into the mud as she took a shortcut over the grass, rather than whether there was someone lurking out there in the shadows.

Jessika jostled the keys in her hand as she crossed to the parking lot, trying to pick out the one that would unlock her vehicle. She fumbled and dropped them, which annoyed her. She didn't want any more delays. She wanted to get home. Ginny and the sofa were calling out for her, a promise she wanted to fulfill.

She stooped and grabbed the keys, catching her heavy purse to stop it from swinging forward and setting her off-balance, then stood still as she turned the keys in her hand again to find the one she wanted. Finally having it ready, with the jangling of the keys still ringing in her ears, she pressed the unlock button and heard her car answer with a beep and a flash.

The flash of light illuminated her, leaving her with the impression of her own reflection in the glass of the window.

A reflection, too, of the man that was standing behind her.

Jessika reacted immediately, throwing her arms out and attempting to make herself as wide and difficult to grasp as possible as she lunged for the door handle. But there was something holding her back – something thin and tight against throat stopping her from bending – something around her neck, she realized.

Too late.

It was yanking her backwards, tightening, and now as her hands flew to it she realized that she couldn't breathe. She was blind again, the darkness even more absolute after that one flash of light, as if it had robbed her of all her senses as well as her breath. She tried to fight, working her fingers against the – what was it? A rope? Some kind of plastic? – around her neck, trying to get them underneath to give herself a little room to breathe. She realized belatedly she was on the ground, her legs flailing out for purchase against the concrete of the parking lot and succeeding in kicking her car. Just for one moment of hesitation she pulled back, not wanting to damage it.

By the time her brain connected the fact that it was okay to damage her car in exchange for saving her own life, Jessika was getting weak. She tried to kick again but her foot only glanced off the side of the car instead of aiding in pushing herself backwards, which she had hoped would put some space between her and the rope. She was fading, her lungs swelling with pain, her head pounding with blood in her temples. She strained, tried to say something, tried to tell him, no, not like this, please. Tried to say her wife was waiting for her at home.

No words came, no breath to carry them. Jessika fought a little longer though she felt herself fading, everything going somehow darker, colder, her legs and hands no longer responding the way that she expected them to. She kicked one last time and found she had no strength to lift her leg again, no strength at all, and her last disappearing thought was about Ginny sitting with that bottle of wine and the pasta on the stove, wondering what on earth was keeping Jessika so long tonight.

CHAPTER TWO

"Well?" Laura asked, looking into Chris's face with a swell of nervous hope she wasn't sure she should feel. He hadn't immediately cast her hand away and told her to get out, or accused her of being mad, the moment she'd said it.

"I'm psychic. I have visions of the future, which I'm not able to control. Mostly I see really terrible things, and then I have to try and stop them from happening. That's why I'm good at my job. That's why I do what I do. And that's how I was able to save Amy from your brother."

He'd tensed, his hand moving slightly on top of hers, but that was all. The only reaction he'd given. And now, the way he was looking at her, she had to wonder whether he'd even heard her. He looked like he was waiting for more.

"I don't get it," he said, at last.

"Don't get what?" Laura blinked. She thought she'd been clear. But then again, it was a big revelation. Maybe he needed a bit more time to process it. She could go through everything in more detail if he needed it – perhaps tell him exactly how the visions worked.

"The punchline," Chris frowned. "I don't know if I'm just being stupid, but I can't work it out."

"There's no punchline," Laura said slowly, a bad feeling growing inside her stomach. "I'm not telling you a joke."

"Well, you are, though," he said. "Aren't you?"

Laura blinked again, looking at Chris for what felt like the first time all of a sudden. His handsome, friendly, open face. The brown hair that seemed to sit somewhere on the intersection of neat and unruly, like he just simply didn't have the time to care about styling it given how busy his daily life as a cardiac surgeon and newly minted guardian of a young girl was. Somehow, it only made him look all the more charming. And yet, that open, honest, friendly face suddenly seemed to be closing off to her.

"I'm not joking," she said faintly, and this time she was the one to slip her hand out from under his, feeling awkward now about the contact.

5

She'd feared this so much. She'd even had a nightmare about him finding out and calling her deluded, having her committed for her psychosis. But she wasn't making any of this up. She really was psychic, and she really had used her visions to save Amy from her abusive father and deliver her into Chris's guardianship.

This was only the second time she had ever told someone, and she wasn't good at it yet. This wasn't going the way she had wanted it to – not at all.

"This isn't very funny, Laura," Chris said, his tone turning firmer than she had ever heard it before. "I asked you to be honest with me about what was going on in your life – what made you pull a gun on me when I went to help your friend Zach with his heart attack. I don't appreciate you trying to turn this into some kind of prank."

"I'm not – it's not…" Laura took a deep breath, closing her eyes for a moment and then starting again. "It's not a prank or a joke. I'm serious. I saw a vision of you stabbing Zach and I didn't know what to make of it. It was foggy around the edges – I didn't know it, but being near Zach was actually messing with my visions and obscuring them. When I saw you go to stab him in real life it was like my worst fears coming true. That's why I pulled my gun – I was panicking."

"Are you serious?" Chris asked, though given that she'd already answered that once, she felt it must have been more of a rhetorical question. "That's inappropriate. You know about… about my brother. I don't find that funny at all." He was leaning back from her now, physically pulling away, like he didn't want to engage with her anymore.

Laura did know about his brother. She'd been the one, after all, to have Governor John Fallow arrested. She'd been the one who had seen the visions when she touched Amy's hand, and seen the little girl's horrific death. She'd been the one to rush in there and save her, even though she'd been warned by her superiors – by people outside of the FBI, even – to leave it alone.

She knew all about John Fallow and his violent rages, and that was why it felt even more shocking that Chris really thought she would use it as a joke.

"I'm not trying to be funny," Laura insisted. "Chris, I need you to listen to me right now. I am deadly serious. When I touch something, I sometimes get a vision from it – of something that will happen. Sometimes it's nothing important, like a waitress dropping a glass and smashing it. But sometimes I see murders. I use the information I see in my visions to intervene and stop them from happening."

Chris frowned, staring at her. "You *are* serious, aren't you?" he asked.

"Yes," Laura said. She reached for his hands, but over the kitchen island that divided them, he was too far away – and he didn't reach back. "This is what I'm trying to tell you. When your brother – when he did what he did, I saw it. I saw it happening to Amy. That's why I ran in there. I wasn't supposed to. I didn't even have a warrant. But I knew something was going to happen to her if I didn't go in. I saw it! That's how I knew to go in there when he got violent!"

Chris looked at her in silence for a long moment. She was about to add more to her plea just to fill the space when he spoke again. "I was told you were hanging around outside the house because you'd got into some kind of vendetta with John. That you'd been warned not to, but you did it anyway, and you heard the screams. I put it down to you being concerned about Amy. I figured you'd seen the signs of abuse enough times to know it when you saw it."

Laura bit her lip. This was the problem with carefully constructing reasonable lies that people would believe, so she didn't have to admit that she was psychic. The more believable the lies were, the harder it was to undo them.

"That's what we told people," she said. "To make it all make sense. I couldn't admit the truth."

"Laura, you're not making sense now," Chris said. "Just think about it. When we first met, you told me you wanted to keep an eye on me because you wanted to know that Amy was alright. If you had these so-called psychic visions, wouldn't you know that I would be fine?"

"It doesn't work like that," Laura told him, knowing that she must sound ridiculous. "I can't just make them happen at will. I can try, but it's not as simple as that. And anyway, I might not see the right part of the future – no matter how many times I saw Amy being happy with you, it wouldn't prove that she wouldn't also get hurt."

Chris sighed, passing a hand over his forehead. "You've been under a lot of stress at work lately," he said. "The burn on your hand, the concussion you had, this case and the damage to your throat – should you even be talking this much?"

Laura's hand strayed to her own throat. The angry red marks were still there from her attempted strangulation by the last serial killer they had faced down. "I've been drinking a lot of hot drinks with honey," she said, which wasn't really an answer.

"Laura…" Chris sighed again. "You've got to take better care of yourself. This isn't good for you. You've been working too hard without a break, and that blow to the head you took can't have helped. You need rest."

Laura shook her head. "I'm not delusional, Chris. This is real."

Chris bit his lip, regarding her with an expression of deep concern. "I don't know what to think," he said, almost to himself, before raising his voice back to a normal level. "Laura, I think you should see someone for help. I have a friend from work who could probably fit you in, even though it's short notice."

Laura stood up, backing away. "I can't speak to anyone else about this," she said. "There's only two people in the world who know – you and Nate. I'm trusting you with this. You can't speak to anyone about me."

"I'm worried about you," Chris said. "Please, just think about it? What you're saying is… it's ludicrous. Fantasy. If you really believe all this, then you need to get help."

"No one, Chris," Laura said, backing away a few more steps. "Promise me."

Chris hesitated.

"Please," she begged. "Don't tell anyone what I said. Please. This could ruin my life, my career, if you tell people that I'm crazy. Promise me."

Chris sighed heavily. "I don't want to do anything that would hurt you," he said. "I promise I won't tell anyone else. For now."

Laura narrowed her eyes.

For now?

"I should go," she said, feeling the panic rising up, clawing at her insides, and bubbling up her throat. "Forget I said all of this. I'm going home."

"Okay," Chris said. He didn't get up to see her out. Laura thought of the layout of the house in her mind's eye, and she wondered. Was he staying to form a protective barrier between her and Amy's room? "I think that might be for the best."

Laura turned and walked out as quickly as she could, braving the cold December air to rush toward her car, and it was only when she was parked in the underground lot for her apartment building that she finally gave into it and began to cry.

CHAPTER THREE

Laura looked at herself in the mirror, tracing a hand over her neck where the marks had been. They were faded completely now, and she was able to tie her blonde hair back in a ponytail again as she habitually did without giving Lacey any reason to worry about her mother.

"Mom," Lacey called from behind her. "Stop looking at yourself."

Laura chuckled, shaking her head as she turned. "You're so bossy," she said. "Why can't Mommy look at herself in the mirror if she wants?"

Lacey looked back at her with that matter-of-fact confidence that five-year-old children innately seemed to have. "Because Mommy needs to feed me," she said.

Laura laughed out loud this time, shaking her head. She moved over to the coffee table where her daughter was sitting with a coloring book and a bundle of colored pencils, ruffling her hair. "You're hungry, baby? It's a bit early for dinner."

"I could have some ice cream," Lacey said hopefully.

"It's the middle of winter," Laura shook her head. "Try again. Something healthy, maybe. What about some carrot sticks?"

Lacey made a face. "Why does it have to be healthy? It's Christmas."

"Christmas was two weeks ago," Laura reminded her.

"You said that when I came over we could have Christmas together all over again so we didn't miss having it together," Lacey reminded her back, her voice very much holier-than-thou. "And Daddy let me eat unhealthy stuff when it was Christmas."

"Did he, now?" Laura asked, bending down to prepare for a surprise attack.

"Yeah, we had cake and pies," Lacey said, completely oblivious – until she started screaming with laughter as Laura tickled her.

"If you want cake, you've got to do some exercise first!" Laura told her, laughing as Lacey squirmed and squealed and tried to get away.

"Mommyyyy!" she howled, her high-pitched laughter filling the whole of the small apartment, until Laura finally stopped and sat down next to her, out of breath herself.

"When are we gonna go see Amy?" Lacey asked, once she had calmed down.

Laura paused. It was difficult to explain to a five-year-old that Mommy and her new boyfriend – Chris – were having an argument and that she might not ever be able to see her best friend again. Then again, maybe Lacey would understand all too well. She knew what it was like to have her parents get divorced, after all. She had almost been too young to remember, and Laura hoped that when she was grown up she would forget entirely about the separation, the court case for custody, the fact that Marcus had kept Laura away from her for so long.

But even so, she couldn't put her through that again. Not right now, when everything with Chris was so new anyway. She hadn't even told the girls that they were seeing one another – as far as they knew, they were just getting to have a lot of fun playdates.

"Amy's having a second Christmas, too," Laura said. "She's busy with Chris. They're having some family time, just like us."

"We could have family time together!" Lacey exclaimed.

Laura resisted the urge to facepalm. Trust the logic of a five-year-old to get around any roadblocks you might try to put in the way.

"They just want to be together on their own," Laura said. "Just like you and me."

"But we aren't even doing anything special," Lacey protested.

Laura bit her lip. "We opened your present this morning," she said.

"I had loads of presents from Daddy and Nana and Grandpop. We opened them on Christmas Day."

Laura felt resentment bubbling up inside of her, and it took everything she had not to snap at Lacey. Marcus had been the one who threw her out and left her with nothing in the divorce, taking advantage of her alcoholism to argue that he needed the full share of the house and all the things they'd bought together to look after Lacey. And Laura had been on a downward spiral, too out of it and too low to argue. She'd spent years since then rebuilding her life slowly, including this shabby apartment with all the second-hand furniture.

As much as living on an FBI agent's salary was a lot better than plenty of other professions she could have tried, it wasn't a magic pill. She wasn't instantly rich again, or even out of debt, just because she had a good job. She couldn't afford to match the amount of things Marcus and his family could buy for Lacey, and her own parents were long gone.

She was never going to be able to measure up to what they could provide.

Except maybe for the distant hope that Chris might accept her, might show her that her trust in him was not misplaced. Might bring her and Lacey into his family and accept them, too. Laura could see herself and Lacey happy in that big house. Not because it was big, not because Chris was well-off, but because he was a good father to Amy. A good man. He would be a good father to Lacey, too, and a good husband.

Or would have been, because Laura wasn't sure that was in the cards for them at all anymore.

"Okay, well, we can't go see Amy," Laura said, getting up and going into the kitchen just so that she could try to let some of that frustration go.

Lacey whined, but Laura didn't respond, and after a few moments the little girl went quiet. She made a kind of harrumphing noise and went back to her coloring, which almost made Laura cry. She was such a good girl. She hardly ever made a fuss, and even when she did, she would accept being told to stop. And Laura was here being the best mother she could be, and still letting Lacey down at every opportunity.

Laura took the chance of her relative privacy at the kitchen counter to look at her phone, opening and checking the message thread she had with Chris out of paranoia that she had somehow managed to miss a notification. But there was still nothing. No answer to any of the texts she had sent him over the past couple of weeks, beyond a terse and nondescript *Merry Christmas, Laura.*

No reassurance that he hadn't told anyone else and wasn't going to. No agreement to meet and talk it over some more. No acknowledgement that he might still have feelings for her after what she had said to him.

She'd risked it all, and it felt like she had lost.

Laura turned back from the kitchen with a small packet of candy in her hand, feeling bad about not giving her daughter ice cream and bad about giving her the candy. She felt bad about everything.

It was days like this that made her miss the bottle so badly she could walk right over to the store and buy whatever they had in stock. But she didn't. She was looking after Lacey right now. She had to stay strong, be responsible. Even if she ever was going to fall off the wagon, she absolutely couldn't do it while Lacey was staying over with her.

"Thanks, Mommy," Lacey said quietly, taking the candy and then humming a little tune as she opened the packet and took the first bite. Laura watched her silently for a while. Sometimes it felt like there wasn't much to her life beyond being a mother and being an FBI agent. If she lost those things, who would she be? Did she even have an identity of her own anymore, or was she relegated forever to just her job and her family roles?

Her phone buzzed in her hands, and she somehow wasn't surprised at all to see that the only person who thought it was worth calling her was her boss. Chief Rondelle's name was flashing up on the screen, and she answered it with a sigh.

"Chief," she said, keeping an eye on Lacey in her peripheral.

"Agent Frost," Rondelle said. Thankfully, there was an edge of softness to his voice today. Far too often lately, he'd been in such a foul mood that when Laura and Nate went in for briefings they'd felt like they had to run and duck to avoid being targeted. "I'm sorry to disturb you on a weekend, I know it's an important time for you. Are you with your daughter today?"

"Yes, I am," Laura said. "But what is it?"

Rondelle hesitated, but he clearly didn't let it stop him for long. "I have a case for you and Agent Lavoie," he said. "Something that fits your specialties."

Laura resisted the urge to sigh. That meant more than one body, it meant weird and unusual details, and it meant a case that 'normal' agents would take months to solve.

But Laura wasn't normal, and that was why they had gained a reputation for being able to tackle those difficult cases.

"How many dead so far?" she asked.

"Two," Rondelle said. "It's tough, according to the local police. There's no connection between the two women apart from the murder weapon. They -"

"Alright," Laura said, cutting him off. She didn't know how much of the conversation Lacey would be able to overhear from this proximity. It didn't matter, anyway. "I'll be there in a couple of hours."

She could have pretended that she wasn't going to go. Tried to turn Rondelle down. Only, if she did, she knew exactly what would happen. Rondelle would tell her that the case was really important, that only she and Nate had the experience and skills to take on a case like this.

And truly, what else was she going to do? Spend another week sitting around, going into the office to do paperwork and prepare statements and testimonies for upcoming trials, thinking of clever ways to cover up her abilities under cross-examination? Sit around at home on her own in the evenings, stewing over the fact that Chris still hadn't talked to her? That she was alone again now that Zach, the only other psychic she had ever met, had gone back home for the good of both of their abilities?

No. The last thing she needed was more time alone with her thoughts.

She put the phone down, then looked at Lacey. Her daughter was already looking back at her with a serious, pouty face. "I'm going back to Daddy, aren't I?" she said, sulky enough to be a teenager already.

"Yes," Laura said, and hesitated. "That was what you wanted, really, wasn't it? To go play with your new toys at Daddy's house and eat whatever he lets you eat?"

Lacey shrugged and went back to her coloring, and Laura took that as confirmation.

Even her daughter didn't want to spend the weekend with her when Laura was feeling this way.

It felt like all she ever did was let her daughter down. But what was she supposed to do? There was no one else who could save these lives. No one else who could do what she did and get the results so quickly. If she didn't go, she was sentencing someone to death – someone's daughter, or sister, or mother, or wife, or girlfriend. Someone who was loved and cared for just as much as Lacey was.

And Lacey wasn't in danger. In fact, out of all the various disagreements they'd had, one thing Laura couldn't fault Marcus for was being a great Dad.

Laura picked her phone backed up and dialed. As if he'd been worried that something would happen to his daughter while she was away from him, Marcus picked up immediately.

"Marcus," Laura said, not letting him start. "I've been called in for a job. I need to drop Lacey off with you."

She bit her lip, calculating in her mind all the steps she needed to get to the J Edgar Hoover Building – the FBI headquarters – in time for her briefing.

She would make it – she always did. When lives were on the line, Laura wasn't going to hang around.

They had a case to solve, and she wasn't going to let it slip out of their fingers to go to a less competent team.

CHAPTER FOUR

Laura got out of the car with a kind of shaky feeling in her legs and arms, a nervousness that reminded her of being a teenager. She'd made exceptionally good time in packing Lacey up and dropping her off with Marcus, who had met her halfway since he was already out of the house. It had given her an extra fifteen or twenty minutes, depending on traffic, for the last leg of her journey.

An extra fifteen or twenty minutes that had turned her wheel in this direction, to stand in front of the same door that had made her feel a similar level of nervous a couple of weeks ago.

She hadn't been able to get in touch with Chris since that day. She was sure he was reading her messages and seeing her calls. They weren't so much missed as ignored. But she had to try, at least, before she left for some other state for who knew how long. There was always a chance she could be out working on a case for months, though with Zach gone she thought she might be able to rely on her visions coming back to make it quicker.

She'd already had a few that seemed stronger and more predictive than before. They only warned her about a vase about to get knocked down from a wall and a burned turkey on Christmas Day, but at least they'd been strong, clear visions of the kind that she used to have before Zach appeared in her life. It was a good sign.

So, maybe she would be back in town sooner rather than later. But leaving without at least trying to say goodbye wasn't a chance she wanted to take.

She took a breath and knocked hard on the door, trying to sound confident and authoritative. The sound echoed just slightly through the hall of the house behind it, and Laura strained her ears for footsteps. Even the sound of him coming to the door, seeing her through the peephole, and leaving again would be fine. Anything, to give some indication of what she could expect from him.

If she thought he was there, she could at least shout her goodbye through the door.

But there was nothing, and long minutes stretched out into silence. Laura stood on her tiptoes and tried to strain to see through the

14

decorative glass panels at the top of the door, putting out a hand onto the door itself to steady her as she did so. A headache pulsed through her head, and she dropped down onto flat feet –

Chris was in medical scrubs, wielding a scalpel with a look of intense concentration on his face. Laura watched this side of him she had never seen, the thin sliver of his face visible between his mask and the cap he wore, both of them blue. His eyes were darting around sharply, utterly focused on the task at hand.

There was a loud beeping noise and his eyes shot up, a frown on his face. Laura felt herself moving back a little as if zooming out a camera; she saw him poised with the scalpel, other people rushing around him, forced into motion by the beeping, calling out medical terms she didn't understand.

"What's happening?" he asked. "He shouldn't be reacting like this. What's going on?"

"I don't know," someone else replied.

"Did you check his notes for allergies?" Chris asked, in the tone of someone having to ask whether a person had remembered to wash their hands before eating or put on their underwear before their outer clothes.

"We didn't have the notes," someone else said. "He came in through emergency already unconscious. We didn't even know his name until right before we started."

Chris stood back from the table as someone shouted "clear," his scalpel held high in the air to avoid injuring anyone or getting in the way. The man on the table in front of him was shocked by another member of staff – Laura, with her vision centering on Chris, couldn't see who.

"The records have just come through," someone said, bursting into the room. Chris turned to look, along with a couple of others. They bent their heads over printed notes.

"Who do we have?" Chris asked.

"George Elwood," one of the nurses said, but he was already halfway down the document, reading ahead.

"There," Chris said. "Damnit! We have an atropine allergy!"

There was more chaos and movement then. Even Laura, who was used to being around first responders, had no idea what was going on. Several members of the medical team were shouting back and forth at one another, listing the names of different medications and procedures at such a rapid pace that her head spun.

15

Chris had put down the scalpel and seemed to be scrambling with the rest, though what he was doing, Laura couldn't name. "Come on!" he shouted from time to time, but as time ticked on, it began to be clear that what they were doing wasn't working.

"I'm calling it," one of the other team members said, the others all seeming to stand back, shocked, and weary.

"No!" Chris exclaimed. "How are we going to explain to this man's family that we gave him the wrong drug and killed him? We can't give up."

"He's gone, Chris," the other man replied, sadness in his voice. "It's too late. Even if we bring him back now, the level of brain damage..."

"No," Chris said hoarsely, shaking his head. "God. This man... he came to us for emergency help."

"We let him down," the other man said. A bloody glove rested on the side of Chris's scrubs, on his upper arm. "But it's over."

Laura blinked, the vision dissipating from her mind like smoke. It had been clear. So clear. And so long. No tendrils of darkness obscuring faces or details, no blink-and-you'll-miss-it duration. A real vision. And by the way her temple was throbbing lightly now, she knew it was a vision for some period in the future: perhaps a day, two days, even three.

She thought about it. She could say nothing. Go on to her case. Chris didn't believe her, anyway. And Nate had expressed a fear that even if Chris did believe her, he would want to study her rather than support her.

But then she would be partly responsible for a man dying. And if she could help, she should. And more than that: if Chris saw her vision come true and realized she was telling the truth, they might be able to continue having a relationship.

It was a big risk. If he did believe her but still didn't accept her, he could still go to her commanders, try something that would cause her to lose her job.

All Laura had to ask herself was this: Was Chris worth it?

He hadn't been answering her texts. Maybe he wasn't even reading them. But Laura knew he didn't work on Sundays. He was out somewhere, probably with Amy. He would have to come home before tomorrow when, she guessed, the vision she had seen was going to take place.

She delved into her pocket and pulled out her notebook, finding a blank page and quickly writing on it. She tore it out, then studied her message for a moment before pushing it into the crack between the door and the frame until it was wedged there. Chris would have to see it when he came in. Then he would know.

She turned and went back to her car, taking one glance at the door and giving herself the chance to change her mind once she was behind the wheel. She didn't want to change her mind.

She started the engine and sped off towards HQ, trying not to think about Chris anymore and focus on the case instead, knowing that whoever had died deserved her full attention.

***

Nate looked up as he got out of the car, hearing a screech of tires that he somehow recognized. Maybe it wasn't the sound of the tires themselves but the timing of it, and the knowledge that Laura would be arriving around now, but he knew it was her before the car took another screeching turn and zoomed over to park next to him.

He lifted a hand in greeting, leaning against the bumper of his own car as he waited for her to get out and join him. "Hi," he said. "I'm surprised. I thought it was your weekend with Lacey."

"It was," Laura said, almost breezing right past him, her blonde ponytail snapping from side to side with the rhythm of her rapid walk. "She's gone back to Marcus."

Nate wasn't going to let her get away that easily. "Wait," he said, grabbing her arm and making her slow down so that he could at least walk beside her. "What's going on?"

Laura sighed, shook her head, and shook him off. "I'm just having a bad day, maybe," she said. "Lacey thought my Christmas was lame, and she's probably right. Can't compete with Marcus and his money. I just thought I'd be better off making an actual difference in the world."

"I'm sure you make a difference to Lacey," Nate said. He was trying to reassure her, but he'd never had kids of his own to judge by. He didn't know what the right advice was. Maybe it was better this way. Maybe Lacey wouldn't remember any of this at all when she was older.

Or maybe Laura was on the brink of losing her relationship with her daughter, and he should have told her something different, but Nate was just completely out of his depth.

"Did Rondelle tell you anything about the case?" Laura asked, as they strode together towards the elevators up to the next floor.

Nate gave her a sideways look. "He didn't tell you anything?"

"I didn't ask," Laura said, pushing the button with too much emphasis. "He told me it's our kind of case and we're the only ones who can do it, you know, the normal speech. I thought I'd cut out the time I would waste on arguing with him and just agree to come, since we all know that would happen anyway."

"Alright," Nate said slowly, following her as she practically sprang for the elevator as soon as it arrived. "I guess that's one way to look at it."

"What other way is there?" Laura asked. The elevator hummed, sending them upwards through the building.

"We can say no," Nate said. "Any time Rondelle asks us to do something outside of our normal agreement, we can say no. And yeah, maybe a junior agent would feel pressure to do whatever he asks of them, but we're not juniors anymore. We're a long way from that. We could probably pick and choose our cases as much as we wanted."

"Right, but if we say no, that means we're leaving people to be murdered when Rondelle puts agents on the case that won't work as fast as we do." Laura sighed, shaking her head as the elevator came to a stop, the doors whooshing open. "You know as well as I do that we're the only people who could ever find the answer to some of the cases we work on."

"You mean, you're the only one," Nate said, unable to stop a trace of bitterness in his words. He regretted it as soon as he spoke, but it was too late to take it back.

Laura bit her lip, but he could see that she did mean that, yes. She just didn't want to say it.

"I have a responsibility," she said, instead. "If I have this power, I ought to use it to save people. You know how I feel about the work we do."

Nate sighed, following behind her as she sped up ahead towards Rondelle's office. Clearly, she wasn't interested in discussing it further, because she was walking right towards the area where Rondelle might be able to overhear them talking.

Nate kept his mouth shut. Talking about this any further would only risk getting Laura in trouble if their boss ever found out that she thought she was psychic. Of course, Nate knew now that she really was – but other people would think she was just crazy. He wasn't going to risk anyone else hearing it because of him, especially not if it wasn't something that Laura wanted.

He couldn't help but wonder what had her in this kind of mood, though. The last time they'd spoken about personal stuff, on the way back from their last case, Laura had said she was going to tell Chris the truth about her abilities. She was serious about him, Nate knew. But then there had been a break over Christmas – and they'd actually had a break, this year – and then they had been focused on getting caught up on paperwork and testimony, and then...

And then, today.

Had Chris rejected her? Refused to believe her?

Nate wouldn't be surprised. He'd done the same himself, at first. He was more concerned with Laura and how she was taking it. If she was going down some self-destructive spiral, like she had when alcoholism had ruined her entire life, he needed to do something.

He just didn't exactly know what, given that he hadn't been able to stop her back then, either. He'd offered to help her with Chris, and if it came to it he would testify to him on her behalf, but she'd said that wasn't necessary.

Laura knocked at Rondelle's door before Nate even finished walking over, and at his terse command, she opened the door and stepped inside. Nate had no choice but to follow her, even though what he really wanted to do was to make her stop and talk to him – and maybe persuade her to go back home, call Marcus, tell him it was all a mistake, and she could take her daughter for the rest of the weekend after all.

He found himself standing in front of Rondelle's desk instead, waiting with his hands clasped respectfully behind his back for their commander to speak. Rondelle was an imposing presence, despite his age and the fact that he was smaller in stature than Nate himself. The salt and pepper grayness in his hair did not take away from his impressiveness – it only underlined the many years of his life the man had given in service to the FBI.

And as for the fact that he was smaller and wiry – that just gave Nate the impression of the kind of boxer who could easily knock out someone in the weight class above his own.

"Agents," he greeted them, barely looking up from his desk. "I've got your briefing notes here."

"Great, sir," Laura said, stepping forward with her hand out. "What time is our flight?"

Rondelle looked up. Instead of handing her any documents, he looked right through her with the kind of piercing stare that always made you think he could see right into your soul and everything you had ever done wrong. Selfishly, Nate was glad it was Laura getting that stare and not him. He didn't want to face it.

"You don't even know where you're going," he said.

Laura's hand snapped closed on nothing and she pulled it back – almost as if to say she wasn't going to get fooled by an empty promise twice. "Wherever you want us to go, of course."

Rondelle shook his head at the clever answer. "What's going on, Agent Frost? Normally you argue with me about each case. And you definitely don't normally take them when it's your weekend with your daughter. I was expecting to have to strong-arm you into this one, maybe promise some extra pay or bonus annual leave days."

Nate opened his mouth to say he'd take both or either option, if they were still on the table, but Laura spoke first and cut him off.

"I knew you would win eventually, anyway," Laura said, much the same as she had to Nate. "Besides, sir, you're our boss. You tell us where to go, and we go there. That's how it works. I like my job."

Rondelle actually threw his head back and laughed. "The number of times you two have pulled whatever stunt you liked, demanded anything under the sun, and done things your way and no one else's… we both know that's just crap. Tell me the truth, agent. I don't want to send you into the field if it turns out you're not mentally fit for it."

Laura squared her shoulders. For a moment, Nate thought he was going to have to dive between them to break up a fight. He wasn't even sure who to put his money on to win. Rondelle had the build and the type for it, but Laura… when she was backed into a corner, he'd never once seen her fail to come out on top.

Admittedly, most of the time, it was because he was able to come to her aid before anything really bad happened. But it wasn't like he wouldn't have her back even here.

"I had a fight with my boyfriend," Laura said through gritted teeth, and the startling honesty of it made Nate's jaw drop open. "I'm mentally fine, I just don't really have the Christmas magic floating around in my head anymore and I wouldn't mind getting out of town and getting some space. And like I said, this is my job and I actually like it. If someone's murdering people and the locals can't solve it, then we should."

Rondelle cocked his head at her for a long moment, like he was deciding whether or not to believe her. Finally, without looking away, he reached for a folder lying on the left-hand side of his desk and picked it up, holding it out to her.

Laura took it as he started talking.

"We've got two dead women in Nevada," he said. "To answer your question about the flight, you've got two hours to get yourself to the airport. It's a six-hour flight, roughly, so once you arrive in the early morning and drive to the town you'll have to hit the ground running. The city of Annabel is a few hours' drive from the airport."

Nate groaned. "There's nothing close? Not even a private airstrip?"

"Afraid not," Rondelle said, although Nate could easily have interpreted that more as *not on our budget* than *not on the map*. "The two victims came just two days apart. One was found this morning, but killed last night. As I'm sure you can work out, that means by the time you land and get to Annabel, we'll be expecting another victim before the end of that night. Time is of the essence, to put it mildly."

"Any connection between the two victims?" Nate asked, though of course he had very little hope it would be that easy.

Rondelle looked at him with just the hint of a twinkle in his eye that said the same thing. "Nothing that the locals could find," he said. "They were both strangled from behind with a very specific weapon – though we haven't identified what it is, it's sharp and strong. Whoever this killer is, they've used it to almost garotte the victims. There's no chance for the women to get their fingers underneath it – and if they do, it's strong enough to simply crush or even cut their fingers."

"How do we know that?" Laura, who had the benefit of flicking through the crime scene photographs, asked.

"Forensics," Rondelle said shortly. "Everything else you need to know is in the briefing package. Names, ages, last seen, and so on."

"We know what to do," Laura said, flipping the folder closed and putting it under her arm as if to indicate that she was done with the conversation. Damn, Nate thought – she was feisty today.

"Then you'd better go and get ready for that plane," Rondelle said, which was as good a dismissal as any.

Nate once again had to scramble to keep up and follow Laura out of the door. If she kept going like this, he thought, it was going to be a very interesting case.

And by interesting, he meant difficult.

CHAPTER FIVE

"So," Nate said, settling into the passenger seat and slumping down, extending his legs until his knees hit the underside of the dashboard. He was still a little out of it from the sleep he'd managed to get on the plane, and glad that Laura had volunteered to drive this time. "Tell me about Chris."

Laura's eyes only flickered over to him for a second before she refocused on the road. "There's nothing to tell."

Nate scoffed. "Come on, Lau. You know I'm not going to give up asking. We're stuck together for as long as it takes to solve this case, and you can't get away from me. You might as well just tell me now."

Laura gave a short, sharp sigh of frustration, and for a moment Nate thought he'd pushed her too far. "Fine," she said, then, and he relaxed a little. "I told him. Like you said I should."

Nate squinted, on the alert already. That wasn't a good start. Now it was his fault, whatever had happened. "Well, I mean, you said you wanted to. I was just taking back my advice to *not* tell him. I didn't force you to do anything. It was your own choice, you know."

"Relax," Laura sighed. "It was my choice. I know that. I just kind of wish I hadn't made it."

"What happened?" Nate asked.

"I told him, and he didn't believe me. And then he started to believe that I believed it, which was somehow worse."

Nate sat up a bit, not at all liking what he was hearing. "He thinks you're delusional?"

"Yup. He said I should get help."

Nate really didn't want to say *I told you so*, but he had. This was exactly what he had been afraid would happen. That Chris would think she needed to be on medication. Or that he would tell other people about what she'd said – which could lead to her being committed, losing her job, or even losing Lacey.

There was no point in saying it all again. He'd said it before. Laura knew what his fears were. If she wasn't prepared to listen to them before, then she probably wasn't now. What she needed, Nate could tell, was someone to lean on – not someone to judge her.

"What about since then?" Nate asked, trying to drop himself into more of an agony aunt frame of mind than Laura's constant protector.

"Nothing," Laura sighed. "I made him promise not to tell anyone else, by the way, so don't worry."

"Well, if he does, then like I said, I'll back you up," Nate replied. "We just pretend he was making it all up, and it'll be fine. I'll even pretend I saw him stalking or harassing you, if you want."

Laura chuckled humorlessly. "I think I might be the one who gets in trouble for stalking. I've sent him enough messages this last two weeks."

Nate witnessed. "That many?"

"The only time he replied was to wish me a Merry Christmas, and I get the feeling that was just because he's too nice of a guy to let the holiday pass without saying anything," Laura sighed, rubbing her forehead. The road was reasonably open, stretching on through desert on either side of them with not a town in sight, and only a couple of other vehicles. She could afford to take a hand off the wheel.

"He'll get back to you when he's ready," Nate said, shifting back down into his seat again.

"Will he?" Laura asked. She glanced at him sideways. "I mean, really – will he? I don't even know what men think. He just went silent on me. Would you do that if you were planning to get back in touch with a woman later on and carry on seeing her? Just ghost her completely for two weeks?"

"He didn't ghost you completely," Nate pointed out. "He wished you a Merry Christmas. He wouldn't have done that if he never wanted to hear from you again."

"You think so?" Laura asked. She was biting her lip, drumming her fingers on the steering wheel. Nate thought she probably didn't even know she was doing it. "What if he just did that thing where you select all of your contacts at once and just hit send to all?"

Nate chuckled. "People still do that? I thought that went out in the 2010s. Maybe even the 2000s."

Laura shot him a look. "Our generation used to do it. And Chris is older than me. Maybe he still does it."

"I don't know," Nate said, shaking his head. "Just… give it a little more time. It took me long enough to come around, and I've known you for longer than he has."

"Hmm." Laura clearly wasn't satisfied with his explanation, but she had nothing else to say. Nate huddled down further in his seat, wishing he was still asleep.

"I don't wish I hadn't told him," Laura said softly.

Nate glanced at her. She was staring straight ahead at the road. "Yeah?"

"I needed to tell him. Just like I needed to tell you." She sighed deeply. "I just wish it didn't always go so badly."

"I'm sorry."

"What for?" Laura asked, her gaze straying to him for just a moment in surprise.

"Not… believing you. And when I did believe you, not wanting to be around you." It was Nate's turn to sigh heavily. "I should have had your back from the first time you told me."

"We've gone through all of this," Laura said. "It's done. I forgave you. And you forgave me for lying for all those years. It's done."

"I know, I know, I just…" Nate shrugged. "The more time goes on, the more I wish I'd reacted differently back then."

"It's water under the bridge," Laura said softly.

Nate let it go. He wasn't going to stop feeling guilty just because she told him to, and going on about his guilt wouldn't make her feel any better. But it was clear to him now that he had messed up way beyond how much he thought he had. If she thought that everyone in her life was going to react this way – and the results would justify that so far – then she was going to end up closing herself off to everyone around her even more than she already had.

"Hey, Lau?" Nate asked, settling further into his seat, and wishing he could just pull a blanket over his head and ignore the world today.

"Yeah?"

"Wake me up when we get to Annabel."

***

Laura nudged Nate on the shoulder, shaking him gently from side to side. He made a noise of complaint somewhere deep in his throat but then opened his eyes, squinting into the morning sun.

"We're here," she said.

Nate groaned in response, but then sat up in his seat, blinking his eyes rapidly and giving himself a shake. "Crime scene?" he asked.

Laura nodded ahead. "I parked a little way away so no one would see you waking up, Sleeping Beauty," she teased.

Nate chuckled. "Thanks. I've got you on the way back to the airport, by the way."

"You better hope we fly at night, then," Laura said breezily. "Or you're going to end up owing me one. You ready to go take a look?"

Nate reached up to his neck, probably to try and work out whatever kink he'd managed to put into it by sleeping in the car. Admittedly, Laura had slept on the flight just like he had, but by now she was used to the contortion required to put yourself to sleep in a plane seat. A car was something different. She figured Nate was going to have muscle kinks on muscle kinks for the rest of the day.

Much better to have been the driver than to put yourself through that.

"Yeah, I'm ready," Nate said. He reached into the back to grab the jacket for his black suit, opening the car door and standing up to put it on. Laura got out of her own side, standing, and shading her eyes against the sun to look at the crime scene in the near distance. It was the middle of winter; the sun wasn't supposed to be this bright. But there it was.

They were in a large parking lot which adjoined a number of local businesses: on one side, a superstore with sliding glass doors that were swishing open to admit new customers even as Laura glanced around. On the other two sides, smaller businesses lined up in neat rows. Across the third side was the road, and over it, another small block of office buildings. There were a few police officers standing around outside one of them, in uniform, but most of them were clustered around something at the far side of the parking lot they were in, closer to the road. Laura focused her gaze on that cluster and, after a glance at Nate to make sure he was ready, began to stride towards it.

The closer they got, the more she could see. There was police tape around an area that encompassed quite a large portion of the parking lot, which she approved of – though it was possible it needed to be even wider. A single car was left inside the tape, a car which had to be hiding the scene from them.

"Who's in charge here?" she called out, getting close enough for them to not only hear her but also see the badge she was holding up.

"Oh – hi!" someone replied, quickly appearing in front of them. Nate strolled to a stop beside her as Laura did, looking the person who had greeted them up and down. She was Hispanic, maybe in her late

25

thirties, and way too cheerful and smiley for both this time of morning and a crime scene. "I'm Sergeant Cortez. I'm in charge of the case – although, now you're here, I guess you're in charge of the case!"

"We are," Laura said, somewhat reluctantly. There were two types of local law enforcement that she didn't get on well with. The first was the ones who were antagonistic to her presence or ambivalent about their jobs – the kind of people who got in her way by being negative. The second was those who were so enthusiastic about their jobs they ended up getting in the way, too. And Laura had a feeling about Sergeant Cortez.

"We've been making sure the crime scene is prepared for you," Cortez said, somewhat breathlessly. "Please, come and meet the team. These are the detectives assigned to the case – you can ask them for whatever you like."

Laura looked at the group of six men and women with a sigh. This was going to be a lot of trouble. "Names?" she asked, already feeling weary.

"Ronnie Grey, Greg Lyon, Connor Judd, Rebeccah Andrewson, Jasmina Tanzi, and Zak Stanford," Cortez rattled off. Laura immediately forgot all their names, assigning them a sobriquet in her head: old detective, frat bro detective, cool detective, curly-haired detective, princess detective, overweight detective. She decided to remember Tanzi and Judd if she needed to call on someone for help. She wasn't going to remember which ones they were, but at least she would have a name to shout. She'd met far too many people in this job already.

"This is the crime scene?" Nate asked, thankfully moving the topic onwards.

"Yes!" Cortez exclaimed. "So, this is where the victim was found. Obviously, her body has now been removed to the morgue. We believe that she was about to get into her car when she was attacked. It was unlocked, and the car keys were found not far from her body."

"Theft is not a motive, then," Laura pointed out.

"Definitely not, ma'am," Cortez nodded. "The victim's purse and phone were still on her body, as well as items of jewelry."

Laura nodded. She turned to Nate, who was a comfortingly normal and everyday presence when there were so many new people to contend with. "Opportunity, or target?" she mused aloud. It was less of a question than a statement. Those appeared to be the two possibilities here. Either someone knew what time their victim would leave work and waited to harm her near her car, or it was a case of a killer walking by and seeing someone who would make a good victim.

"Surveillance footage?" he asked, glancing around at all the nearby businesses.

"Um, we have taken a look," one of the detectives spoke up, almost shyly. The curly-haired one. "It was dark last night, and the attacker was wearing a dark hoodie over dark clothing, the hood pulled over their face. It's hard to pick out on the footage where they came from – they just disappear into a part of the lot where there isn't enough light and then they're gone, and we don't know where they came from or if they had a car parked nearby."

"Alright," Nate nodded. It was bad news, but then again it was good that they'd been looking into this kind of thing themselves. If the locals were halfway competent, it would make the case that much easier. "We'll at least be able to get an idea of their build from the footage. Do you have the images?"

Someone reached into a pocket and pulled out a cell phone. The frat bro detective. "Yes, sir. Right here." He handed over the phone – a flashy, newer model – and Nate flipped through a couple of stills before showing it to Laura.

The man on the footage was hard to make out, but he was a man. That, Laura could tell. He was taller than the victim and had much broader shoulders. There was also something in the way he stood, the way his hips moved when he walked, that spoke to masculinity. As always in these kinds of cases, though there was still a very slim chance that the murderer might be a woman, it was hugely improbable according to statistics. For her to have the build and walk of a man, and to kill like a man, would make her incredibly unique.

They assumed a man, then, and that was what they would stick to.

"What about forensics?" Laura asked.

"Ah, well, not everything has been processed yet," Sergeant Cortez spoke up. "But so far there hasn't been a lot of evidence to go on."

"What do you mean by not a lot?" Laura asked. "Some, or none at all?"

"None at all," Cortez admitted, looking chagrined. "The area didn't yield any particular items of significance on our search. We found the victim's personal possessions and car keys, but they only held her fingerprints, and the murder weapon hasn't been found. All we know is he didn't use his hands, because there's a dark line across the neck – we thought the throat had been cut, at first, but there was no external blood."

"For the first victim either?" Laura clarified.

"Nothing for her, either," Cortez replied. "That's where this case is starting to get tricky."

Laura nodded, looking around the crime scene as she thought. The killer must have either parked nearby, or come from behind one of the neighboring businesses. What was behind there?

"What about the murder weapon?" Nate asked. "You said it looked like blood, but wasn't? So, what was it?"

"An imprint." Cortez looked a tiny bit green as she looked down at the ground, at the place where the victim's body must have been laying. "Around the neck, it's… it's deep. So deep you can see the impression of the material. Our coroner identified it. I guess they've seen it before. I'll let them explain it to you."

Laura looked up towards the three sides of the parking lot again. "I'm going to walk the scene," she said, looking at Nate.

He nodded, clearly understanding that this was both a notification and an invitation. "I'll make sure all the bases were covered," he said.

Laura walked away and left him with the group of detectives, glad to do so. She worked better alone and always had – with Nate being close enough to her now that he almost counted in her being alone. Having to brief and drill seven extra people was her version of a nightmare.

But there were many more questions to be asked, more boxes to check off. Had they gone door to door and spoken to everyone who owned or worked in the businesses? Had they canvassed for witnesses from passersby? Had they started going through the security footage and eliminating all the people who had been seen in the area, or all the cars that could be identified? Had they interviewed family and friends, started combing social media pages?

Nate was more than capable of finding out all the answers to those questions himself. Laura had a suspicion that this team knew enough to have done those checks, and she wasn't expecting them to have found many results. After all, when you could easily handle and solve a case yourself, you didn't have to call in the FBI.

Laura walked across the parking lot alone, feeling the chill of both the January morning wind and the thought that she was walking in the footsteps of a killer, possibly. There was no telling where he had come from – unless she could find some evidence now that would shine some light on it.

As soon as she was out of view of the gaggle of detectives, going down an alleyway between two buildings, Laura put out her arm and trailed her fingertips along the brickwork, hoping that maybe the killer had leaned on the wall as he passed through and she might trigger a vision.

She walked all the way around the back of the buildings on three sides of the parking lot before she gave up. Laura knew it had been worth the try, but in the end, all she'd been left with was sore fingertips and weariness from sitting for so long and then walking for so long so early in the day.

She walked back towards Nate, who was shading his eyes and lifting a hand with a wave, with an uneasy feeling that this case might be harder than any they'd recently faced – especially if her visions were still not working.

And if they were never going to work the same way again thanks to all the prolonged contact she'd had with Zach…

It   didn't   bear   thinking   about.

CHAPTER SIX

Laura looked up as Nate pulled into another parking lot, this time behind the local precinct. They had followed Sergeant Cortez all the way here in her patrol car. She had a kind of déjà vu whiplash: the feeling of always doing the same thing over and over again and never really getting anywhere. Every case seemed to be the same. Every precinct had that same kind of parking lot, every time they came into a new town it was the same song and dance routine.

Maybe she was just getting jaded. Or maybe everyone that always told her to take a break now and then was right. It wasn't like she was going to listen to them, anyway.

"Let's get on with it," she said wearily, and Nate shot her a concerned look as she got out of the car which she summarily ignored.

"This way," Cortez called out to them, beckoning from closer to the building. Laura held back a sarcastic comment about being able to see the door with her own eyes and followed her in silence, pushing her hands into the pockets of her black pants and keeping her head down.

She and Nate passed through the doors of the precinct and into a noisy space. A bullpen faced them, with members of the public sitting in the area outside of it – most of them likely waiting for loved ones to be signed out with the desk on the right. Cortez led them to an elevator which they piled into, and they rode up in uncomfortable silence to the fourth floor.

"Here it is," Cortez said, with far too much false cheer, as the elevator pinged and the doors swooshed open. She stepped out into what was clearly a more familiar space, her demeanor becoming more confident immediately, and led them right over to a desk. "This is our witness."

Laura stepped around Cortez and looked down at the man in his crumpled suit. He looked like he had been at the precinct all night, though they must have let him go and then called him back in for this discussion. "You found the body?" she asked.

"Yes," the man answered, nodding in a kind of stunned way. He must have still been processing the whole thing. "I found her in the parking lot when I was leaving work."

"Tell me what you saw," Laura said. There was a chair at the desk, and she took it, shutting out Cortez so that she could focus.

"I was just walking across to my car and I saw something dark on the ground," he said. "I thought it was a bunch of clothes or something. Anyway, I thought it was strange. I turned on my cell phone screen so I had some light and looked again, and I realized it was – her."

Laura nodded sympathetically. "Can you describe to me what you saw?" she asked. There were crime scene photographs, but there was always a chance something had been moved and disturbed. And in times of great stress, people often noticed small details that they wouldn't have otherwise.

"She was lying there, on her back. No, sort of on her side a little. She had her eyes open. Like she was looking at the sky, only she looked scared."

"Where were her hands?" Laura asked.

The man closed his eyes for a brief second, remembering. "Around her – on the ground. Like she was reaching up, but only as far as her own shoulders. There was a weird kind of ring on her finger, too."

Laura pictured it in her mind's eye. The victim trying to grab at her own neck, to loosen the noose, while the killer strangled her. She was lying on her back, but her arms were still up, so he hadn't done it while she was standing up. He had dragged her down to the ground, fought and choked her there, then pushed her dead body off himself and onto the ground. Her arms flopped down onto the pavement, but stayed raised.

And there were no forensics?

She looked up at Cortez, who was standing close by as if waiting to be useful. "Tell your coroner to check the victim's hair for fibers," she said. "She would have been in close contact with the killer."

"Right," Cortez nodded smartly, clearly heading off to do it immediately.

"This ring – what do you mean by weird?" Laura asked.

"Well, most women wear a ring with a gem, or just plain silver or gold wedding rings," the man said. Laura felt a subconscious twitch of her own ring finger – the one that had once worn Marcus's ring and was now bare. "This was made of wood or something. And it had this kind of interlocking pattern, only it was… broken or something."

"It's with the coroner, along with her other items," Cortez supplied helpfully. Laura nodded and set that aside for later.

"Did you see anybody else nearby? Any cars?" Nate asked.

The witness shook his head. "There were a few cars parked nearby, but nobody in them," he said. "The office buildings – they can be accessed twenty-four-seven, so I guess people stay there all night sometimes to get work done. Or maybe it's people who live nearby leaving their cars there, I don't know. But there's always a few vehicles left at any time of night."

Laura nodded, thinking. The murder site was basically a fishbowl. Enclosed on all sides by buildings full of watchful eyes – both human and digital – and yet no one had seen a thing.

Either this killer was very skilled, very knowledgeable, or very lucky.

"Is there anything else you can think of that might be relevant?" Laura asked. The man shook his head no.

"Alright, then, sir," Nate said, gesturing to him. "You're welcome to go. I'm sure you have a life you need to get back to."

He nodded gratefully and disappeared.

Once he was gone, Nate looked at Laura with a raised eyebrow. Their next step was clearly obvious to both of them. "Bodies?" He suggested.

"Bodies," Laura agreed, getting up and preparing to head to the morgue.

***

The morgue was, thankfully, downstairs in the basement of the precinct, meaning there was no need to travel far. Nate led the way ahead of Laura as they walked down the stairs, into the cool, white, sterile environment. There was a hint of bleach in the air, and two white-coated lab techs sitting at a table in front of a number of scientific-looking machines.

"Hello?" Nate called out. "Is one of you the coroner?"

"Oh, yes," the older man said, standing up. He had gray-peppered dark hair and a neatly kept beard, and rimless glasses that glinted light in their direction when he stood up to greet them. "You must be the FBI agents."

"Agent Lavoie and Agent Frost," Nate said, gesturing to himself and then to Laura. "What can you tell us about the bodies?"

"Right down to business, then," the coroner said, clasping his hands together. "I like that. Well, we can tell you a lot about the killer's MO. Both of the victims were strangled from behind and showed minimal signs of struggle – a couple of broken nails, some light damage to the fingers, and a bruise or two on the legs or back. It appears to me that he approaches them from behind and manages to get the ligature around their necks with the element of surprise, allowing them little time to fight and no chance at running."

"We can assume he's fairly strong?" Laura asked.

"Oh, yes, definitely," the coroner said. He gestured them over to one of the drawers at the back of the room, opening it, and pulling back a white sheet to reveal the body of a woman. "You can see from the ligature marks around the neck here that he is very consistent. It's a thin line with no variation, see? That means he was able to get it around the neck and keep it in the same place, no slipping around. Though they will struggle to get free, he's strong enough to hold the ligature in place and prevent them from even so much as budging it."

"And the murder weapon?"

"I would say it's a thin plastic tie, reinforced for other uses so that it doesn't snap when he pulls it tight," the coroner said. "There are no fibers or imprints of pattern, so it's a smooth material and very strong. However, it's a little thicker than a professional garotte and doesn't leave any trace of metallics on the skin. That's how I've come to think plastic ties. I've seen them before – very, very strong. Wrapped around a gloved hand, they wouldn't break."

"Any clues that would help us identify him?" Nate asked.

"I can tell you his height and build, though I gather you already have that," the coroner said, glancing at her over the top of his spectacles. "Another characteristic of the ligature mark tells us that he is taller than both of his victims so far. I think it's important to note that the bruising sustained is light to medium, rather than heavy. They will have sustained it from kicking and flailing around and coming into contact with things, not from dropping down heavily. While he does drag them to the ground to strangle them, he doesn't simply drop them. It's all very controlled. He keeps them inside his grasp, no chance to roll away or flip around on him."

Laura took an unhappy breath. He was the kind of killer who left his victims with very little opportunity to get away. In general, serial killers weren't known for their mercy or for wanting their victims to have a fair chance to escape, but this was brutal. No chance at all to stop him from killing them as soon as he had his plastic rope around their necks. That was it. Done.

"Did you get the message about the hair?" Laura asked.

The coroner nodded. "Yes, Sergeant Cortez was down here just a moment ago," he said. "I'm afraid I'll tell you what I told her. We have already done extensive checks of that kind. On both victims, we did find traces of black fibers, but there's nothing we can do to help identify him with that. It's a generic cotton blend with a very common type of dye, and you already knew he was wearing black from your security footage."

Laura sighed. Why did they always have to be so complicated?

"We heard something about a ring," Nate said.

"Oh!" The coroner turned with a grin and produced a wooden ring, held in his gloved hand. "It's ingenious, actually. A puzzle ring, used as a wedding band. We managed to get it back together."

Laura frowned, examining it. She put out a hand but the coroner jerked it away.

"Don't touch anything, please," he said. "I'm still running tests, so I may need to retest the ring or any part of the bodies and the things they came in contact with in order to get another sample if the first one doesn't come back with any results."

"Of course," Laura said. She probably looked like a stupid rookie for trying to touch evidence, but it had been a plot to try to trigger a vision, and now she had no way to excuse it. "You said it's a puzzle ring – can you demonstrate how it works?"

"You have to touch it in the right order," he said. "One, two, three – there. I think it must have come undone unintentionally in the struggle, just by accident. Now, you see the pieces and how they line up?"

He tilted them, and Nate let out an exclamation. "It's a message!"

"My one and only forever," the coroner read out. "It's a bit of a generic message to hide in such a clever ring, if you ask me, but there you are. A declaration of eternal love is pretty appropriate for a wedding band, I suppose."

Laura wondered which of the couple was the one that was into puzzles – or whether it was both of them. She wasn't sure yet whether it had any relevance to the case, but it was something to ask the other half about. Especially if there was a chance it hadn't come undone by accident. Had Jessika been trying to send a message?

"Anything else you can tell us?" Nate asked.

"Not much, I'm afraid," the coroner said. "No explained marks or injuries, nothing that links the two of them together."

He pushed the body back into the drawer, leaving Laura's hand twitching by her side. She hadn't had a chance to try to touch the body and see if it would trigger a vision, especially with his warning hanging in the air.

"Well, thanks anyway," she said, resigned to the fact that there was no natural or unsuspicious way she could try to touch one of them now. "Keep us updated if anything else should come to light."

"Of course," the coroner nodded. "And let us know if you have any more leads, too. Even though we weren't able to bring anything new from the hair tests, it might be that the next tip you get will lead to something."

Laura nodded, allowing herself to smile at the coroner. He was obviously more experienced in his job and was pleasant with it, a good mix. It wasn't his fault that he hadn't been able to shed any further light on the situation.

"Well, I guess we have some family members to go interview," Nate said, by way of escaping the conversation, and Laura nodded. They did, at that.

Though she couldn't say she had any extra special hopes about finding anything new, given that Cortez and her team actually seemed to be good at their jobs – which meant that the usual routes of inquiry most likely weren't going to be enough for her and Nate this time. They were going to have to work harder if they wanted any shot at catching this killer.

CHAPTER SEVEN

Laura settled onto the open spot on the couch next to the grieving widow, looking her over with concern. She was obviously still in shock, sitting almost mute and incredibly still, and she was so pale and shaky it was clear she needed a careful hand.

"It's Ginny, isn't it?" Laura asked, trying to ease her way into things. She accepted a hot cup of coffee provided to her by a hovering and anxious mother. The woman had the look of someone whose loved one was hurting, with nothing they could do to stop it. It was a very particular pain that Laura hoped never to experience.

"Yes," Ginny said, almost distantly, before her eyes snapped onto Laura and she seemed to focus at last. "Geneveive Granger. Jessika is – was -" She stopped, choking on the past tense.

"Your wife," Laura filled in, because that was the positive part of the sentence, the part that Ginny needed to remember and focus on. That the relationship was and had been, and that was cause for celebration. It was going to take her many years to get over the grief enough to accept that, Laura knew, but if she could help her take one step on the journey, she would.

"Yes," Ginny said. She sniffed loudly and then stopped, almost as if the sound had startled her out of crying.

"Can you tell me anything that might help us figure out what happened to her?" Laura asked, phrasing it gently so as not to startle her in another way. "Or who did it?"

"I just don't understand," Ginny said, her voice going distant again. She was shaking her head slowly. "She just went out to work like normal. She was going to come right home. We just had Christmas."

"I know this is hard to take in," Laura said. She was frustrated but also incredibly sad for this poor woman. They needed answers, but Ginny had just lost the person she thought she was going to spend the rest of her life with. Maybe getting direct with some more specific and easy to answer questions would help. "What did Jessika do for work?"

"She's a therapist," Ginny said, stumbling over the tenses again. There was an added lightness in her face when she started to talk about her wife's work, as though it made her happy and proud. "She specializes in trauma – people who have been through really awful experiences, usually when they nearly die. It's quite common for people like that to experience PTSD or other forms of traumatic response. Jessika helps them to work through it."

"Cognitive Behavioral Therapy?" Nate asked from his spot in the nearby armchair.

"For the most part," Ginny nodded. "She keeps a few other tricks up her sleeve for patients who need more help. Oh… what will happen to them now?" She looked up at her mother as if for reassurance.

"I'm sure someone else will take them on, dear," she told her daughter. "Don't trouble yourself with that."

"But they need her," Ginny protested, and Laura's heart broke just a little because she knew where it was coming from. Because Ginny was saying that *she* needed Jessika.

Laura hated doing family interviews so much.

"Her patients," Nate said. "Did she ever have any that became too attached? Or perhaps any that became angry with her or raised disputes?"

"I don't think so," Ginny said. She looked up at Nate as if she hadn't noticed him before. "She's not allowed to talk about that kind of stuff. It's confidential, you know? Patient privilege. She never said she was afraid or that anyone had been awful. She just carried their weight – their traumas. I don't want you to look into them. I can't imagine they would hurt her, and she would hate that. To have negative stereotypes fall on her patients. She cared for them so much."

Laura nodded. She figured that in some ways it would be hard to tell the difference when you were around someone who worked in that field. Was she having a bad day personally, or was she just moved by the story of someone she had been treating?

And even as she nodded in agreement, she was wondering why Ginny wanted to ignore a possible avenue of investigation. Wouldn't she want them to leave no stone unturned? Wouldn't she want them to make sure they found out who did this, no matter who it was?

"Jessika was wearing a very interesting wedding ring," Laura said, by way of introducing a new topic.

"Oh, yes!" Ginny reached out her own hand, showing an identical ring. "We loved them. It was a little nod to our love of puzzles and escape rooms. That's what we did on our first date – an escape room."

Laura nodded. That explained that. "Is there any way it could come open on its own?" she asked.

37

"Open?" Ginny frowned. "No, there's no way. You had to press it a certain way. Jess learned how to do it with the same hand she was wearing it on, but that required a lot of practice and twisting her hand a specific way – and pulling the ring halfway up her finger, too. It's not something that could happen by accident."

"Then why would it be open?" Laura asked.

"It was..." Ginny's face paled, then colored, then fresh tears came to her eyes. "Oh, God. She must have wanted me to know... wanted to show me that... that even though she's gone..."

It was a fair explanation, but it was also one that threatened to derail the interview. Laura knew they had to change the subject before Ginny burst out crying and couldn't recover.

"What about..." It was delicate, but Laura had to bring it up. "Anyone, whether a patient or otherwise, who had a problem with your marriage?"

Ginny looked at her blankly.

"With the fact that you're gay?" Laura prompted.

Ginny shook her head. "Not specifically," she said, which spoke to a whole lifetime of discrimination that couldn't be pinned down to just one occasion.

"You can't think of anyone who would have wanted to hurt her?" Laura asked.

"Never," Ginny whispered, and she looked so lost that Laura wasn't surprised when her mother moved to put her arms around her.

"I think that's enough for now," Ginny's mother said, looking pointedly at Laura as if she was the one who had caused the grief in the first place. "Don't you?"

"Alright," Laura said, but she took out a business card and laid it on the table. Ginny was in shock now, but as the shock wore off, maybe something would come to her mind. "If you think of anything..."

There was no response from either of the women. Laura looked at Nate and raised her eyebrows; he nodded in agreement. The two of them stood and went to leave. Laura lingered in the doorway for a moment, feeling like she should say some kind of formal goodbye – but Ginny was sobbing quietly now into her mother's shoulder. Laura bit her lip and walked away, leaving the house by the front door, and hugging herself tightly against the cold while Nate closed it behind them.

"What do you think?" Nate asked.

"It's worth looking into her patients," Laura said. "We need to get access to her files and also find out if there were any police reports from the last five or even ten years about harassment or violence towards her. She saw emotionally volatile people at work every single day. We wouldn't be doing our jobs if we didn't start there. And Ginny's insistence that we not look at them... to me, it just makes me want to look even harder. Maybe she knows something about one of them that she doesn't want us to."

Nate nodded. "Agreed," he said. "It makes me suspicious, although there's a chance she really is just reflecting what she knew her wife's wishes would be. And even if we find something that looks off, we're going to need to find some link between any suspect and the other victim, too."

"One bridge at a time," Laura said. "Let's get back over to that office."

***

Laura pulled a file folder from the bookcase and opened it, looking inside. "Nothing in here," she said. "It looks like admin."

Nate sighed. "I didn't know we were going to have to do an escape room as well as solving a murder today," he complained.

Laura chuckled. "Well, the door's open, so I don't think this counts," she said. She cast another look around the room, trying to think. "It has to be in here somewhere, doesn't it? Cortez said there's only a car key and a house key on the keychain she was found with. Unless the killer took the key to the file cabinet, it has to be in here."

"Right, or she wouldn't have been able to access her own files," Nate said. He had a thoughtful look on his face. "I'm not ready to give up and assume it's been taken yet. Let's keep looking."

"Look where?" Laura raised her hands in frustration. "It's all just books about psychology and stupid ornaments!"

"Well, maybe we can figure it out somehow," Nate said. "They loved puzzles, right?"

"Right..." Laura glanced around. What was it Nate had just said – that this was like being in an escape room?

What did they do in escape rooms?

She looked at the shelf closest to the desk. It was full of books about psychology: *Unlocking the Inner Secrets of the Self, New CBT*

Techniques for the Modern City, Case Studies: A Look into Near Death Psychosis...

Wait. Unlocking secrets? Laura grabbed the book and then paused. Was that... a clunk she'd heard?

Laura opened the front cover of the book and looked inside. It was hollow, with a cut-out box rather than actual pages. In the middle of it all was a small silver key.

"Thank God for that," Nate grinned. "You're lucky today. Make sure to touch as much stuff as possible in case you get a vision."

Laura rolled her eyes at him and took the key out. It had nothing to do with luck. "Let's just see if it actually fits the lock before we start to celebrate," she said. She tried it in the file cabinet's lock and turned it – and with an audible click, all four of the drawers rocked very slightly, released from their trapped positions.

"Can we celebrate now?" Nate grinned, coming over to stand beside her.

Laura opened one of the drawers fully and thumbed through the files inside it, suppressing a groan. "Only if your preferred mode of celebration is to go through hundreds of files about therapy patients," she said.

"What a wonderful coincidence," Nate deadpanned, reaching in and grabbed a whole bunch of the files at once and taking them over to a small coffee table in front of a sofa.

Laura grabbed the rest from the drawer and thumped them down heavily on Jessika Granger's desk. She sat down in the chair, casting a look over her shoulder at the other three drawers they hadn't even opened yet in despair, and opened the first one to begin reading.

Each of Jessika's patient files was well-organized into a standard structure, which was a plus. There was a front page with a photograph, some basic information and contact details, and a diagnosis with space for medication details. These had been filled in with a looping hand, which was much easier to read than that of many medical professionals Laura had come across. That was another blessing.

Thank you, Jessika Granger, Laura thought, and began to read.

The files all told a very similar story. Almost all the patients that Jessika took on, just as Ginny had told them, were involved in some kind of terrible accident or had a medical emergency that left them at risk of losing their lives. As a result, they'd ended up with mostly diagnoses of PTSD: flashbacks, new anxieties and fears, intrusive thoughts, nightmares. Almost all of them, too, had undertaken courses of CBT, just like Nate had predicted.

Every file seemed to have the same arc. They came to Jessika, she diagnosed and treated them, and they got better. Some of them were managing their symptoms well enough to leave her service after months, others after years, but most of the files appeared to be closed. Only a handful were current patients – which made sense, given that Jessika was working alone and only had so many available hours in her workday.

"This is useless," Laura complained, dropping the last file onto the pile, all of them unhelpful. "All I'm getting from this is that she was a really great therapist who managed to cure almost everyone she met."

"I don't think it's a case of curing when it comes to this kind of mental health issue," Nate said mildly, flipping through another page of the file he was reading. "It's more ongoing treatment until it reaches a manageable level."

"You know what I mean," Laura sighed. She dumped her pile back into the drawer, opened the one below it, and groaned. It was just as full as the first. "This is going to take us all day."

Nate picked up his cell phone without taking his eyes away from the file, glanced at the screen once to check where the buttons were, and the put it to his ear. "Hi, Sergeant Cortez? Yeah, we're at the therapist's office. Yeah, Jessika Granger. If you could send a couple of detectives over to help us go through some files, that would be appreciated. Mhm. Thanks."

He put the phone down without missing a beat in turning the page of the file, carrying on as if he hadn't even paused in the first place.

Laura watched him for a second and then sighed. He was right, obviously, about that being the best course to take in order to ensure they got through all the files quickly. Maybe she just wasn't used to working in a city where they had a force capable enough of doing these kinds of tasks. She definitely wasn't used to having her own taskforce. They only got to bring in a team when things were really difficult and they'd been working on it for a while, which never happened for Laura and Nate.

Delegating was, apparently, not part of her skillset. It hadn't even occurred to her as a possibility.

The detectives must have been nearby already because Laura had only managed to get through three more files before there was a knock at the door. She got up to answer it, honestly glad of an excuse to not be looking at the files for a moment because it was already feeling like her brain was going to melt out of her ears. Nate, on the other hand, had barely stirred at the sound of someone at the door. He was completely absorbed in the files.

Laura opened the door to see the two detectives she had requested – Cortez had sent frat bro cop and princess cop, which made her nervous. She hoped that she was wrongly judging books by their covers. If their personality types matched their looks, they might not end up making it quicker to get through the work after all.

"Hi," she said, anyway. She didn't bother trying to greet them by name – she knew there was a very low chance that she was going to get them right. "Come in. We're checking through the patient files for signs of anyone who had violent tendencies, who had a grudge against Granger or was disgruntled with her services, anyone who showed worryingly obsessive behavior towards her, that kind of thing."

"We'll get right on it," princess detective replied, dropping onto the sofa that was clearly normally used for patients as frat boy detective followed Laura to the file cabinet to grab some.

Laura sat back down at the desk, but she found her attention wandering now that she knew there was someone else going through the paper files. Maybe she would have more luck doing something else, like… looking through the computer, for example.

She placed her files on the coffee table for the others to go through and then booted the machine up, waiting for it to load impatiently. She flipped through the notebooks on Granger's desk and found nothing – only torn-out pages. She traced the outline of letters on the uppermost page of one of them and thought she could make out general patient notes: *Brian finding more success with new techn. – call with mother – no nightmares 2 mos – anxiety at work.*

So, if she was reading things correctly, Granger's method had been to make pen and paper notes during the session, then type them up, print them out for the files, and tear off and throw away the originals. No; Laura saw a shredder by the desk. She shredded her original notes to preserve client confidentiality. She was conscientious. Laura wondered if she would be turning in her grave – or, at least, turning in her drawer at the morgue – over everyone going through the files now.

The computer screen blinked to life – showing a login box requiring a password. Of course it did. Laura drummed her fingers on the desk for a minute, thinking. Granger was a sensible type and very security oriented. And yet, in a room that was very carefully devoid of her own personality, there was one personal object in sight. It was a photograph of herself and Ginny on their wedding day, both of them smiling in ivory gowns with floral crowns. They were standing next to a sign: J & G – 8/29/. One of their dresses covered the year, but that was enough to guess.

Laura typed in 'Ginny829' and held her breath.

The screen cleared onto a desktop, and she gave herself a victory grin.

She started clicking through folder after folder on the computer, to the background noise of the others turning their pages in a symphony of gentle swishing that seemed to go on so constantly they couldn't possibly be reading everything properly. Laura stopped looking into the patient folders after a cursory examination of a few revealed them only to contain the same information Granger had ultimately printed out for the files anyway.

Another file that beckoned was interesting: some kind of briefing document, it looked like, saved onto the desktop directly. Laura opened it up and realized it was a list of her policies as a therapist. She scanned down it, seeing directives about how to make payment, what to do if you needed to miss a session…

And then, halfway down the list, a note that made Laura groan out loud.

"What is it?" Nate asked, his attention snapping to her immediately.

"I found her policy for new patients," Laura said, spinning the chair around to look at the three others in the room. "She doesn't take on patients with a history of violent or criminal behavior."

There was a heavy sighing all around the room.

"That doesn't mean we won't find anything," Princess detective pointed out. "They might have become violent or obsessive after she started treating them."

Nate shrugged. "She's right. We should still keep looking."

"I agree, but I'm less optimistic," Laura said. She turned back to clicking around on the computer. There was an email inbox which was depressingly neat and tidy: it looked like Granger only used it for patient communications, and almost everything was incredibly benign. Booking and rebooking appointments, sending copies of files or instructions for certain therapeutic strategies, alerting her whole patient list of an upcoming vacation she was taking.

None of it indicated any level of problem. The emails – both the ones sent and the ones received – all seemed to be polite and even formal in tone. According to everything she read, Laura supposed that Granger had never had an argument with a single patient in her entire time as a therapist.

All of which left them precisely nowhere.

Laura sighed, rubbing her temples.

"Nothing in my files," Nate spoke up at last, breaking the studious silence.

"Nothing here, either," Princess detective replied, apparently having just finished hers at the same time.

There was a long silence. Laura spun the chair and joined both Nate and Princess in watching Frat Bro finish the last file he was going through. He finally put it onto the pile with the others, sighing.

"Nothing."

That was it, then. Their clever idea of looking into Granger's patients had been a bust. And nothing in this office, from the key to the cabinet, the files to the desk and computer, had triggered a vision. Laura was starting to think this was enough evidence to suppose the killer had never been inside the office at all.

"We have to move on," Laura said, even though she was floundering to figure out where she was supposed to go next.

"Back to the first victim," Nate said. "What was her name again?"

"Brooke Ware," Princess supplied.

"Brooke Ware," Nate repeated. "We go back to her and see if there's anything we can discover."

"Do you know where we can speak with her family?" Laura asked, addressing the two detectives.

"We can take you there," Princess replied, jumping up immediately. Like her superior, Cortez, she was obviously eager to impress.

Laura wasn't going to argue with it, or tell her that she had no intention of recommending anybody to join the FBI and never did. With the way this case was looking, it was probable that they were going to need all the eager hands on deck they could get.

She was only too aware of the deadline Rondelle had pointed out: Tonight, the killer was likely to strike again, and they needed to work faster if they had any hope of stopping him.

CHAPTER EIGHT

The second Laura stepped foot into the house, she knew that this family was different.

Where Ginny had been lost in her grief, like a ship trying to sail through fog and ending up crewed only by ghosts, the husband and sister of Brooke Ware were already into a different stage of the grieving process.

Anger.

"Have you caught someone yet?" Jerod Frank, whose name his wife had apparently not taken, demanded as soon as they entered the living room. He was sitting there with what had to be Bree Ware, as well as a detective who looked extremely harassed.

"Not yet, sir," Nate said, stepping in behind Laura. They'd made Princess and Frat Bro stay behind. This detective was one Laura hadn't seen before – probably on family duty and therefore not available as part of the main task force.

"Why not?" Bree demanded. "It's been two days. Two days! They say on TV if it takes longer than two days, you lose your chance!"

"I assure you we haven't missed the chance to catch the person who did this," Laura said. She and Nate stood at the front of the room, both of them perhaps sensing the need to remain dominant in the space. If they conceded and sat down, taking a weaker position, they would be verbally attacked by Brooke's loved ones until they left.

Laura didn't want to mention the fact that it was now less than forty-eight hours since his last attack, thinking that probably wouldn't bring them much comfort, but it was true. If the old adage about the first two days had any reality to it, they had another twenty-four hours now to get the results they needed. Unless, of course, he struck again tonight, in which case they had even more time.

Not that extending the deadline via the death of another victim was a course of action Laura wanted to take.

"Well, what are you doing?"

"Right now," Nate said, as calmly as possible. "We're here to ask you some questions and see if we can't get some new leads from talking with you about your sister and wife."

"We've already answered so many questions," Bree complained.

Nate raised an eyebrow, a masterful stroke that Laura wouldn't have been able pull off herself. "Are you against answering more if it might help us to find her killer?"

There was a general sense of sheepishness in the room, albeit tempered by the anger that still simmered palpably at the surface. "What is it, then?" Jerod demanded. His tone very much implied that he thought they should have been able to investigate well enough to find out all the answers on their own.

"First of all, we need to know if Brooke had any contact with a woman named Jessika Granger," Laura said, leveling her gaze at the husband and then the sister in order to try and catch them reacting to the name.

Instead, both of them shook their heads slowly and blankly, looking to one another for ideas. "Never heard of her," Jerod said. "Wait – is she the other woman who…?"

"I'm afraid she is," Laura confirmed. "We need to know if there's any connection between the two victims. If there is, it will help us to identify their killer much more quickly. This could be the missing piece of information that reveals everything. Is there any possibility that Brooke might have consulted a therapist or thought about seeing a therapist? Or did she know anyone who was seeing one, to the point of having spoken about it?"

"A therapist?" Jerod snapped. "Why would she need a therapist? Brooke was happy!"

Laura looked at Bree pointedly. If there was something a husband didn't know – or wanted to hide from the police – then the sister might.

"She was happy," Bree confirmed. There was a little less heat in her statement. Like the memory of exactly how happy her sister had been was hard to bear.

"Alright," Laura said, conceding that perhaps these two couldn't shed any light on it. It didn't mean Jessika and Brooke hadn't run across one another at all, or that there was no connection. It could be that they both knew the killer, but they knew him independently of one another. That was entirely possible, but it was also a depressing possibility – she and Nate could be chasing their tails for a long time before they discovered the connection. "Is there anything else you think we need to know?"

"Well, have you looked into that stalker yet?" Bree asked, her voice pointed once more.

Laura exchanged a glance with Nate, then looked at the detective in the room.

"What stalker?" he asked, speaking up at last. "You haven't mentioned a stalker before."

"We didn't need to," Jerod said, hesitating now but not enough to stop his anger. "You already know about him. Brooke filed a police report."

"Why didn't you say anything?" the detective asked, grabbing a cell phone out of his pocket and dialing.

"Because you already have it in your records," Bree said, repeating the point. "Why would we need to tell you about that? You're supposed to know!"

The detective was muttering something quietly and furiously into his phone, retreating into the hall. "It's really important that you tell us absolutely everything, even if you think it's obvious," Laura said, doing her best to keep her voice even. "There's no way for you to know if we've caught something, so you need to tell us every little detail. Who was this stalker?"

"He was a guy she met at work," Jerod said. "She was a barista; he was a customer at the coffee shop. She worked at the same place for the last few years, and I guess he got to liking her too much. He started following her home after her shift ended."

"What happened? Did he ever get violent or aggressive?" Laura asked.

"No." Jerod pushed his chest out. "He came too close to the house once and I let him know he wasn't welcome. Put on a little show for him so he knew she was mine and he had to back off. He never came back after that."

Laura winced internally. That kind of behavior… if this stalker was in the wrong place mentally, it might not have made him back off. It might have made him more determined to 'have' Brooke, by any means necessary. And it also might have just pushed him further back into the shadows to avoid getting caught.

"How long ago was this?" she asked.

Jerod shrugged. "Three months or so."

The detective returned to the room, putting his cell phone back into his pocket. "There's no record of a stalker in Brooke's file. It looks like she did come into the station to make a complaint, but she retracted it not long after. It's there in the notes, but not in her main file – it wouldn't have flagged up automatically."

"She retracted it?" Bree frowned. "Why?"

"The notes say she felt she was mistaken as the stalker didn't return," the detective said. "Are you sure this was definite stalker behavior and not just a coincidence? Was there more than one incident?"

"Oh, yeah, for sure," Bree said. "He was creeping her out for a long while before he started to follow her. She told me she was scared of him. I don't know why she would retract it."

"Maybe she felt bad about making the report?" Laura suggested. "Was she that kind of person? Would she want to avoid getting someone else in trouble?"

"Probably," Jerod said. For the first time, sadness seemed to overpower his anger for a moment. "She was a good person. Really good. I didn't deserve her."

"Don't say that," Bree snapped.

"It's true."

"And now it *came* true," Bree said, looking furious. Like she thought the opinion alone had been enough for fate to do away with her sister.

"Do we have a name for this stalker?" Laura asked. She needed to interrupt whatever pettiness this was – something that could be solved between the two of them – and get to the meat of the matter.

"Floyd something," Bree said. "I always remembered that – Floyd. Sounds like halfway between an old sad man, and that boxer guy."

"Floyd Reedy," the detective said. "That's what it says in the file."

"Right," Laura said. There were more questions to be asked about Floyed Reedy, but they needed to be done away from the listening ears of Bree Ware and Jerod Frank. "Is there anything else you think we already know that you haven't actually said out loud?"

Jerod and Bree looked at the floor. "Nope," they both said, almost at the same time. They looked like guilty kids. They were probably only just now realizing that they themselves had ended up costing the investigation time, just by making assumptions that turned out to be incorrect.

"Then we're going to go and follow this lead and see if it gets us anywhere," Laura said, turning for the door. "In the meantime, please cooperate with the detective here. It's imperative that we have as much information as possible to make sure we don't miss anything."

They nodded, and Laura and Nate walked out of the house with the detective following behind them.

"Do you need me to do anything?" the detective asked, clearly just as annoyed as they were about the way the family members were acting.

"Just keep an eye on them," Laura said. After a moment's thought she added. "And if one of them goes out, try to get someone to watch them. I wouldn't put it past them for one of them to go and try to find this Floyd and take justice into their own hands."

The detective nodded grimly. "Wouldn't surprise me either."

"In the meantime, we'd better go and try to track him down," Nate said.

"You're going to love this part," the detective said. "I asked for his address when I was on the call – I figured you'd need it. Guess where he lives?"

"Where?" Laura asked, her heartbeat jumping in her chest. Was this about to be a big revelation in the case?

"Less than a block from the therapist's office," the detective said triumphantly.

Laura stared at Nate.

It looked like they had a viable suspect already, after all.

CHAPTER NINE

He sat down in the café and took the book out of his bag, taking great care with it. It was so old and dog-eared already, he was afraid he was going to end up knocking the cover right off one of these days. It didn't matter how many times he read it over – each time, he discovered something new. He didn't want to have to carry it around as looseleaf pages because he hadn't taken good care of it.

He placed the book on the table and then saw with chagrin that his sleeve had ridden up. He tugged it back down quickly, hiding the scarring on his left arm. He knew he had been lucky that the damage was only to the surface of the arm and not his nerves or muscles, but it didn't always feel that way. Not when people were staring at him or making comments.

Not when they were saying things behind his back like how it was such a shame, because he might have been good-looking if he didn't have that. They might have hung out with him if it wasn't for his weird scar. If he didn't have that hiding under his clothes, they might have been interested in getting to know him more.

It was always the same.

He sniffed, taking a quick glance around to make sure no one had seen his skin before he hid it, then picked the book up carefully and reverentially. He placed his coffee cup further away on the table just in case someone came by and barged into the table and made it spill. He couldn't risk it going over the book.

"Here's your cake, sir," the pretty barista said, coming by to drop it onto the table in front of him. He gave her a polite but uninterested smile and made sure that was far away from the book, too. He didn't like raising his hopes by smiling at people, these days. And he definitely didn't have time for anything that smiling might lead to, as if it ever was for him.

He carefully opened the book to his current favorite passage and reread it, going over each word carefully and turning it in his head, trying to get a feel for it. These words were important. These words needed to be held individually, then put back into their places, to be fully understood.

Things were like that sometimes since the accident. Needing to take it slow, consider it carefully. But he didn't mind that part. That was something that made sense. Everyone could do to slow down a little more these days – that was what he thought. Not that he had been any different from any of them before.

He shook his head to rouse himself away from old dreams and old memories, pushing them aside. There was no point in clinging onto something that was long gone now. He had to focus.

He read the words one more time, but in reality he was thinking about the next one. He was looking forward to this one. He was looking forward to them all, really. He felt like he was moving his way through a checklist, a to-do list. It had that satisfying feeling one got when finishing a task and being able to cross it off or check the box. It was a good feeling. The kind that triggered the pleasure centers in your brain. He liked to look back at his list, whether mentally or physically, and see that two names were already removed from it. That made him feel like he was getting somewhere.

There was still far enough to go, of course, and it was too early to celebrate yet. But it was good to know that the work you were doing was actually making a difference. To feel those miles still yet to travel starting to disappear under your feet.

He refocused his thoughts as he set the book aside for a moment and sipped at his coffee, bringing the cake closer to take a bite. It was sweet, but nothing would taste as good as getting his whole list checked off. Of course, with any project, once he had finished, there would be another goal to aim towards. But this one would be perfect for now.

Tonight, he was going to check one more thing off his to-do list. His bucket list, even. And it was going to feel so good that the cake was like a celebration in advance – a celebration that couldn't even come close to comparing to the high of the real thing.

CHAPTER TEN

"We're nearly there."

Laura looked up at Nate's words, startled out of her thoughts. "Right," she said.

Nate made a sound in the back of his throat.

"What?" Laura asked.

"Just text him," Nate said. "I mean, you're not up to the level of sending fifteen texts a day yet, right?"

"God, no," Laura said, horrified. "I've sent him maybe ten texts total across the last couple of weeks. And he replied to one, so it's not even ten in a row."

"Okay, so text him," Nate said. "Stop staring at your phone miserably and text him. Then you can get back to the case. Or better yet, give him a call. If he answers, I'll take this interview on my own."

"With a suspect?" Laura said, dubiously. What if the suspect tried to run and Laura wasn't there to help?

"Just stop making up reasons not to and do it," Nate said. "When it's done, you can join me."

Laura decided the best thing to do was what Nate told her, and she hit the call button on her screen without allowing herself to think too much about it.

It was when she put it to her ear and heard the dial tone that the nerves hit her.

What if Chris didn't answer? What if he did answer and told her to go away? What if he blocked her number because she was calling him too often?

The tone rang again. Again. Again.

The voicemail kicked in, telling her in an electronic voice to record a message for Chris for when he got back to the phone.

She canceled the call and sighed, slumping deeper in her chair.

"He's probably busy," Nate said easily, and Laura wished she had his confidence.

In reality, he was probably screening her calls. She'd spoken to him when he was at work before. Outside of actually doing surgery, he had plenty of other responsibilities that kept him in his office – paperwork, training, and all kinds of other things she didn't even know about. And if he was unable to answer at the time she called or messaged him, he always got back to her later.

Always – except for the last two weeks.

He was avoiding her, wasn't he? She already knew that, but – not avoiding: ghosting. That was what people called it nowadays. Laura had been out of the dating scene for so long before Chris that she was almost unfamiliar with the lingo, but she knew that was what he was doing. Just ignoring her, letting her drift away without an answer. She was never going to hear from him again.

This was how things between them ended.

Laura groaned, holding a hand against her forehead. This had all happened because she had been stupid enough to try to tell him the truth. Why had she suddenly had this urge to be open and honest? Lying had worked with her for everyone else in her life for thirty-three years, give or take. Telling the truth to Nate had been an anomaly, but she'd treated it like it was a new rule. What had she even imagined was next? Admitting it to Lacey? To Marcus? To Chief Rondelle? Amy Fallow? Where did it end?

Well, actually, that one was easier to answer. It ended here. She wasn't going to be this stupid again. She was never going to try to tell anyone else. She shouldn't have tried it with him. That kind of foolishness was over now.

"It'll be alright," Nate said, but it was cold comfort. Laura didn't know whether he meant Chris would end up accepting her as she was, or whether he meant she would be fine without Chris. She was almost afraid to ask. "Anyway, we're here."

Laura looked up at the home in front of them. It honestly wasn't what she had been expecting. It was a well-kept home in a good neighborhood, with a small yard out front and a moderately-priced car parked in the driveway. The car itself was sparkling clean as if the owner made sure to take care of it every weekend.

Stalkers, Laura supposed, were capable of emerging from all walks of life.

"Let's go, then," she said. A bit of action would help to keep her mind off things. If they needed to make an arrest, then they would at least not be able to dwell on other matters.

Nate followed her as she got out of the car and strode towards the door, full of sudden purpose that was mostly fake. She knocked loudly and waited, and glanced towards Nate as confirmation that he was bracing himself when they heard footsteps behind the door.

It opened to reveal a man in beige slacks, a button-down shirt, and a knitted vest over the whole ensemble, looking like nothing more than the generic nerd that might have been present in any lazily costumed movie.

"Hello?" he said, looking between them with some confusion.

"Are you Floyd Reedy?" Laura asked.

"Yes," he said hesitantly, then seemed to come to a conclusion as to who they were. "Um, I actually already attend a church in the local area, so…"

Laura held up her badge for him to see. "I'm sure that's very lovely for you, but I'm here about your physical crimes, not your spiritual ones."

Reedy, who appeared mild-mannered and retiring, took one look at the badge –

And turned and fled.

Laura cursed out loud, then set off after him through the house, throwing a desperate and silent arm off to the side in the meantime. She heard rather than saw Nate start to run to the left, knowing he'd understood the meaning of her gesture. *Go round the back.* She charged after him as fast as she could, running into a shoe rack at a low level just inside the entranceway and then stumbling on as a sudden headache seized her temple –

Floyd Reedy was running around the side of the house, trying to get away. Laura saw him, his wide eyes set in a terrified face, his arms pumping up and down as fast as he could make them. He glanced over his shoulder but saw no one there, no reason to be afraid. Maybe he was starting to get away. Laura had no idea why she wasn't right behind him, why she was apparently letting him get away –

And Reedy ran full pelt into Nate, who caught him in strong and wide arms that weren't going to let him escape. He clipped handcuffs smoothly and expertly onto Floyd's wrists, first one, then the other, and started to read him his rights.

Laura started to slow down, realizing there was no need for her to try so hard to catch Reedy. Her head was full of stabbing pain now, indicating that the vision revealed a future which was just about to happen. She stumbled slightly on her way to the open back door, holding onto the wall for support as her head stopped swimming so badly. The door had hit the back of the frame with the impact of Reedy running through it, and now it swung back and –

Laura reeled away. There was a hook on the back of the door – probably for hanging coats, but it stuck out at a sharp angle, right at the level of her eyes.

She gasped for breath, clutching onto a small bookcase on the other side of the hall for support, feeling her heart thunder in her chest. If she hadn't had the vision and slowed down – if she had been right behind Reedy as he ran…

That sharp hook would have gone right into her head. Maybe through one of her eyes.

No wonder she wasn't running after him in her vision. She would have been incapacitated at the very least. Given she hadn't heard herself screaming when she had seen Nate make the arrest, there was a good chance she would have been dead.

Outside, she heard a shout and knew that what she saw had happened.

Laura took a breath. She was fine. She hadn't died or been horribly maimed. She was fine.

She stepped out slowly, making sure to avoid the hook carefully, and made her way around the corner to see Nate grinning at her with Reedy in cuffs, shaking his head at her. "You get lost on the way or what?"

She smiled back weakly, trying to pretend that everything was fine. "I knew you could handle it," she said. She could tell him the truth later – she wasn't going to say it in front of a suspect, especially not one who could accuse her of some kind of illegal tactics later.

"Let's bring him in," Nate said, turning towards their rental car – and Laura stretched her arms above her head, grateful she hadn't had to overexert herself, but hoping the headache faded at least a little bit before they ended up in the interview room finding out what Floyd Reedy's deal was.

***

"Alright," Laura said, putting down her cup of water on the table. Every sip of it seemed to temporarily ease her headache just a little bit, which was what she needed in order to get through this interview. "Floyd Reedy. You live on your own?"

"That's right," he said, fiddling with his own hands, folding them over and over again. "What is all this about? I didn't do anything wrong!"

Laura almost wanted to laugh out loud. They always made it so hard for themselves when they did this – and so easy for Laura and Nate. "If you didn't do anything wrong, then why did you run when the FBI showed up on your doorstep?"

Floyd looked down temporarily, studying his hands again and moving his jaw a second before answering. "I heard about what happened to Brooke," he said. "I thought you might jump to conclusions and come and arrest me."

"So you *do* know what this is about," Laura said. "That's once already you've tried to deceive us. You don't seem to be very good at it, Mr. Reedy. If I were you, I would seriously consider telling us the truth. It's going to be easier on you."

"I didn't," Floyd began, stopping himself and then starting again. "I didn't do anything to Brooke. I promise I didn't. I just panicked."

"When did you panic?" Laura asked, leaning forward, and trying to bait him. "When Brooke told you your feelings weren't reciprocated and you lashed out in anger?"

"No!" he said, his eyes wide and horrified. "No, that never happened, I swear! I never even told her about my feelings."

"Well, Mr. Reedy, it seems to me that she would have probably gotten the message when you followed her all the way from work to her home," Nate said. "Don't you think?"

Reedy made a kind of grunt in the back of his throat, as though the memory was unpleasant to him. "That Neanderthal husband of hers certainly did. He punched me in the face."

Nate shifted slightly but didn't lose confidence in his line. "You were stalking his wife. I imagine many men would react the same way."

"I didn't do anything," Reedy repeated. He was pleading with them, his hands open and out in front of him – but Laura noticed with distrust that his fingers were strained and controlled so hard that the tendons in his wrists stood out, every single line of his hands bold and sharp. He was only just hanging onto his composure. How far would he go, Laura wondered, if he was really confronted?

"Where were you last night between six and eight in the evening?" Nate asked. It was an abrupt topic change that they often employed to catch out their suspects – to get them to confess to something they didn't mean to.

"At work," Reedy replied immediately.

Nate raised his eyebrows and looked at Laura, and she met his gaze with a similar expression. "You were at work between six and eight last night?" he asked.

"Yes," Reedy said. "I work in an office, but it's always awfully noisy in there. I spoke with the HR department and they eventually allowed me to change my working hours so I would get uninterrupted time in the evening. I still have to share the space with others for the rest of the day, but I get to go in late, so there's time to relax and have a good coffee before I start."

"A good coffee and a chance to watch her, right?" Nate commented.

Laura glanced sideways at him momentarily. She was starting to get the feeling he was pushing his angle too hard. The answers Reedy was giving were starting to check out.

"Your office," Laura said. "Does it have security cameras?"

"Sure," Reedy nodded. "They cover the entrance and the reception. You can't get out the back of the building without going through reception, either."

They would have to check, of course. There was always a chance he was bluffing. Laura glanced towards the dark glass at the other side of the room over her shoulder, hoping that one of the detectives was standing there and would get the hint to go and get the footage.

"It was Friday night," Laura pointed out. "Why were you working so late on a Friday? You didn't have anywhere better to be?"

"We have a big project on right now. Everyone's doing overtime over the weekend," he said. He glanced at a watch on his wrist. "I should be finishing off the last bits in the office now, actually."

"What about Wednesday?" Nate asked, ignoring his obvious request to leave.

"I was also working then," Reedy nodded.

There was still something that bothered her about him. Laura couldn't tell if it was because she didn't believe his alibi, or because she found him creepy. "Tell us about Jessika Granger," she said. She watched his face closely – but there didn't seem to be any reaction on his face, only a puzzled blankness.

"I don't know who that is," he said.

"You ever had any kind of therapy?" Nate asked.

"No," Reedy said, frowning, looking between him and Laura. "Why should I?"

Laura bit her tongue, and looking at Nate sideways, she could feel him doing the same. This wasn't the time to be giving people free advice about their mental health.

"Do you know anyone who has gone to therapy locally?" Laura asked instead since they needed to get to the crux of this.

"No," Reedy said, shaking his head and screwing his face up. "What is this about therapy? Has someone told you that I do go to therapy? I don't."

Laura rested back in her chair, regarding him wearily. His name hadn't come up in the patient files, after all. It was likely that he was telling the truth about not knowing Jessika Granger.

An alibi for both murders, and no connection to the second victim. It was looking extremely likely that their suspect was not actually a suspect at all.

Yet another dead end.

"Alright," Laura said, getting up and effectively giving up. "You'll need to stay here for a couple of hours while we verify your alibi. If it checks out, you'll be free to go home."

Nate followed her as she left the room, too frustrated right now to stay and go through any niceties. The good thing about being in a city that had a good police force was the fact that she could rely on someone else to do all the usual exit procedures now that he was cleared – or all but cleared.

"Now what?" Laura asked, leaning her head against the wall, too weary.

"I have an idea," Nate said. "But I don't think you're going to like it."

CHAPTER ELEVEN

Laura slumped with her head against the headrest, looking up and frowning. Nate was right. She didn't like this one bit.

"Can't we just go back to the precinct for a bit longer?" she asked. "A couple of hours – tops."

Nate snorted. "No, we can't," he said. He took the keys out of the ignition as if to underline his point. He gestured towards the motel's office, unbuckling his seatbelt. "I'll go and get our keys. Can you get the bags out of the trunk?"

Laura nodded uneasily. She hated this. Going to sleep for hours when there was a killer on the loose always felt so wrong. But she knew the argument by heart already: Nate would say that if they were sleep-deprived, they would have even less of a chance of catching him. The best way to get ahead of a killer was to be fresh and on the ball, ready to act on any clues and put things together. And, of course, any rest she could get now would help with any visions she might be able to bring out tomorrow.

Nate was already at the office and talking to the attendant by the time Laura opened her door, slowly walking around to the trunk and lifting both her and Nate's bags out. They were light, refined down to only the basic necessities after long years of practice. He headed back towards her and she handed one over to him, swapping it for the key to her room.

"Don't look so low," Nate told her. "Remember, rest is a good thing. We're going to get super fresh and in the morning we'll spot something new that we haven't seen before."

"Right," Laura muttered. In her own head, she added: *probably a new body*.

She was reluctant even to turn and follow Nate as he headed towards the rooms. This felt like giving up, in the worst possible way. Rondelle had told them they needed to get in there and find answers fast. And what were they doing? Literally sleeping on the job.

"Come on," Nate called out without looking over his shoulder.

Laura sighed and followed him. There was no point in trying to argue, anyway. He always won these fights in the end. Mostly because, as much as she hated to admit it, Laura was as human as anyone – and, like anyone, she did function better on a bit of sleep. Especially when she'd already had the wind taken out of her sails a little by a vision earlier in the day.

Laura raised her eyebrows in a farewell at Nate, rolling her eyes when he pointed meaningfully at her door while he unlocked his. They'd booked neighboring suites, as usual. When you knew there was a fair possibility that you were going to get up at three in the morning and have to wake up your partner, it was not just practical but also thoughtful to others to be next door.

When he was inside, there was nothing for her to do but follow suit, unlocking the door that had been assigned to her and heading in. She glanced around at the depressingly familiar interior, which didn't have much to recommend it over the hundreds of other motels she had stayed in before. At least the wallpaper was a plain rust-colored covering in this room; sometimes motel owners picked out headache-inducing floral patterns which practically gave her nightmares.

Laura sighed, dumped her bag on the bed, and then grabbed the files she'd snuck inside her jacket and spread them out on the bed as well. Nate could have his way and make sure she checked into a motel room for the night. He couldn't force her to actually stop working.

She chewed one of her fingernails as she went back to the very beginning, going over the first briefing and the initial details again to see if there was anything they had missed. She picked up the crime scene photographs that had been taken of Brooke Ware where she lay, red livid marks around her throat, her eyes open and staring at the sky. She dropped the rest and focused on one to look at it even closer, tracing a finger over the pictured ligature marks as a headache stabbed her forehead, trying to see what she could gain from the –

There was a terrible crashing noise splitting the world apart, the sky coming down on the ground, everything tumbling and moving all at once. For a moment Laura didn't know how to breathe, didn't know how to interpret what was going on. It was like she'd been sucked into an unexpected hurricane, or a plane had crashed into the motel, or –

No. Her world stabilized and she saw what it was. It was a car, now upside down, the sky visible through the lower part of the windshield and everything wrong. The glass was gone, scattered now in winking crystals across the seats, catching the headlights of other vehicles screeching to a stop nearby.

There was someone in front of her. A man. He was older, though his face was obscured by blood, by the crumpled look he had. He was trapped. Laura could see he was trapped. He stirred slightly once and then closed his eyes, opened them again and shut them. Laura heard him groan faintly, a wheeze that went out. A kind of final breath. There were crunching noises of footsteps nearby, shouting voices, lights – but he was gone, his eyes shut, no longer aware of anything around him.

Laura blinked, dropping the photograph. A car accident? What did that have to do with –

The man was walking along a pathway. Laura found her thoughts racing, unable to understand what was happening. A double vision? The same man? Did this vision come before the one she had seen?

He was walking along a pathway in the evening, his breath forming a cloud on the cold air. It was winter – like now, Laura thought. What was this? Was he about to be hit by the car? But in the vision she'd had just now, it had seemed like he was inside the car to begin with when it crashed –

There was someone behind him. Laura saw them, her eyes opening wide with shock, wanting to shout out and warn him. It was another man. A man in a dark hoodie with a cap shading his face – an outfit she recognized – an outfit she had seen very recently on security footage. It was dark here, too dark to catch a glimpse under the cap, his whole face shrouded in shadow – Laura strained to see –

He made a quick movement of his hands and the man, the one Laura had seen die in the car crash, put his own hands up to his neck. He was grasping at something, going down, hitting the floor. Laura went down with him, like a camera that was fixed a set distance in front of his face. She didn't want to watch him die a second time. She wanted to look up – to look into the killer's eyes, to know who he was. But as ever, her vision didn't obey her. Instead, she watched the man struggle and fight, his eyes wide and then popping out, his face going red and then purple as the life was drained out of him.

Laura came back to herself again, her head pounding.

But she didn't know why. Was it because the vision she had seen was of something that was about to happen? Or was it due to the sheer intensity of having two visions at once?

And what the hell had she just seen, anyway? How could a person die twice?

There were so many questions flying around in her head, but first and foremost among her thoughts was that she simply didn't understand what she had seen – and reeling from both a powerful headache and the shock of seeing two violent deaths, she could only hold her head, close her eyes, and groan.

***

Haydn locked up the store and jingled the keys, throwing them up a tiny distance into the air before letting them drop back down into his hand, just once. He didn't know why, but ever since he'd opened the store twenty years ago, he'd always done that after locking up for the night.

He pocketed them and shoved his hands into his pockets, tipping his head up towards the sky for a moment. Did it look like rain tomorrow? He wasn't sure, but for now, the sky was clear and bitterly cold, allowing all the meager winter heat of the day to just rise right up and dissipate up there.

He turned away, thinking about dinner tonight and what he would have and whether it was even so late that there wasn't really time for dinner. One of these days, he was going to stop spending every available hour in the store and actually go out and get a life. He'd left that decision too late for today, however. Maybe too late for this week. There was always so much that needed doing.

Haydn strolled to the car, not so much because he wasn't in a rush but more because he was getting older now and his body didn't respond as well to a whole day on his feet as it used to. He didn't have anyone waiting at home for him, so there was no point in tiring himself out even more just to get back within an arbitrary timeframe. He would shuffle along the street, turn left at the streetlamp up ahead in the distance, walk another five minutes, and then turn in. And then he had the whole of the rest of the evening to rest and not worry about a thing until the morning.

Well, he'd worry about a thing. It was kind of habit by now. He'd run through his routine for the morning ahead and try to remember if he needed to order in any new stock and make sure that the cat hadn't got himself into any scrapes today and wonder if she was going to tomorrow.

There was the sound of a loose pebble scattering across the street behind him. Haydn turned slowly and glanced over his shoulder, wondering if it was a neighbor out for a walk or one of his fellow local business owners maybe also just closing up for the night. He couldn't see anything. He shrugged to himself, continuing on his walk. There were narrow alleys between each building, where most of them kept trashcans. Likely it was a bird or a cat or some nighttime scavenger.

What had he been thinking about...? The cat, that was it. He had to remember to check the litter tray and top up both the food and water bowls before he went to bed or the cat would be up in the morning bothering him before his alarm went off. He always popped home at lunch to make sure Monty, the old tom, had enough to get him through the day. Still, the cat did like a snack in the night. These days, he was probably too old to catch and kill his own prey. Haydn didn't know how many years – or maybe even months – poor old Monty still had left in him.

There was another stone skittering behind him and he looked over his shoulder for another brief moment, wondering. But there was no one there.

In spite of himself, a little shiver ran up his spine. It was nothing, obviously. Just an animal or something falling off a roof, even, that was all. He was only even hearing it because it was so dark out.

He tried to relax, using a technique he often did when he was tired or stressed or feeling like the walk home was simply too far these days. He would think to himself of all the stages ahead of him: he just needed to walk past the fabric store, then the bakery, and then he would be on a stretch of clear road for a while before he reached the residential area of this part of town. He'd walk past the purple house on the corner and turn, and then, and then, and then... the route stretched out ahead of him in small stages, and by the time he'd finished visualizing it all he'd already passed the bakery and crossed off two of those stages.

Haydn took a deep breath of the air and then –

Was that another stone behind him?

Did he have some kind of alley cat following after him, recognizing the scent of an unfamiliar cat on him perhaps?

Or was there something – *someone* – else behind him?

Haydn swallowed, looking ahead only, starting to quicken his steps –

But something jerked him backwards, something thin and sharp against his neck, hitting his skin so hard he almost thought he was cut at first. But then he tried to breathe and knew there was something else wrong – something keeping his throat so tight he couldn't get enough oxygen through –

Haydn was pulled backwards again but he fought, his hands going out ahead of him for balance. He flailed to the side but he had passed the buildings, nothing to grab onto for leverage. He stumbled back two steps and only just got his balance back, and then – yes, of course – he flailed backwards instead, trying to find and hit the person who was dragging him. He wouldn't go down. He refused to go down. He knew if he went to his knees he was done.

Haydn's vision was darkening, his throat constricting, panic starting to flood his brain as his lungs starved for oxygen. He reached back and hit nothing. He thought again. The thing around his neck had to be held by something. If he reached for a hand, he could draw blood, make them stop. He fumbled and reached up, trying to find something and only discovering a slippery fabric – something bunched around a hand but padded somehow – behind that more fabric – nowhere to get a grip, to dig in his nails and scratch or pull – and he beat and pulled at the hands but it was no use – he could feel himself getting weaker – his attempts getting slower – his eyes going dark, nothing in front of him anymore – his chest on fire, then the burning going out – an image, just one image, appearing in front of his eyes:

Monty at home alone, waiting for a nighttime snack that was never going to come, waiting for a scratch behind the ears that he was never going to feel again.

Haydn's body gave out and his mind went after it, leaving nothing behind but an empty shell held captive by a killer.

CHAPTER TWELVE

Laura put the files to one side and lay down, thinking that maybe putting her head on the pillow would convince her to drop off. She lay there for long minutes. A car drove past outside, the headlights breaking through the not quite good enough motel curtains. She tracked the light as it moved across the wall.

This vision thing was worrying. More than worrying. What did it mean that she had seen two deaths? She had thought her power was getting back to normal now that she'd spent some time apart from Zach, but maybe this meant that something was wrong with it again – something more permanent. Maybe being close to another psychic for such a long period of time, before they both worked out that it was the proximity that was the issue, had been enough to screw up her visions forever.

Forever. That was a horribly long time to not have her visions working. To never quite be able to tell if what she was seeing was accurate. To have to double-guess it all.

She might end up just going around wearing gloves and relying on detective work if this continued. She didn't know how much longer she could take the mental pressure. Lying awake in motel rooms and trying to decipher what she had seen. Wishing she could see more. Always feeling like a failure when she was one step behind the killer and her visions just *wouldn't* show her what she needed to see.

Maybe she should call Zach in the morning when he would be awake and around. See if he was experiencing the same thing. But they'd promised not to contact one another for a while to make sure there was absolutely no negative effect lingering. It was still possible, after all, that this was some kind of hangover. Everything working itself out again. Maybe after another week, maybe another month, things would be fine again. And maybe just calling Zach would be enough to set things back off-kilter.

She didn't know. That was the problem. There were so many things she didn't know. So many variables she didn't understand and never had. And if she wasn't able to talk to Zach again, someone who could help her experiment and figure these things out, then she never would.

Laura sat up in the bed and grabbed the files again, yanking the hair tie off her ponytail so the loose hairs would stop bothering her and at least seem deliberate. She opened back up to the first pages and read them for what had to be the seventeenth time, determined not to miss anything.

Her cell phone lit up on the nightstand and Laura reacted without even thinking, grabbing it up and answering the call. She realized belatedly she hadn't even seen the caller ID or the time, but it was too late to back out now. "Hello, Special Agent Laura Frost," she said, which was going to make her sound very silly if it was Chris or Nate or Marcus calling.

"Agent Frost," came the response, and Laura almost breathed an audible sigh of relief. "This is Sergeant Cortez. We've got another body."

Those last words froze her, taking back all the short-lived relief she'd felt, the moment of humor.

Another body.

Someone else was dead.

"When and where?" Laura asked, grabbing her hair tie, and slipping off the bed, shoving her feet into her shoes.

"It's just been discovered, downtown," Sergeant Cortez said.

"Don't move or touch anything," Laura replied, grabbing the files into one big pile with her free hand and then turning for the door. "We'll be there in ten minutes." She ended the call and rushed to go wake Nate, hoping but also dreading that she was about the see the face of the man from her vision again.

***

Laura turned to take in the whole area. Outside the remit of the floodlights all was darkness, but here, in this circle the local officers had set up, the light was almost blinding. It wasn't dissimilar to the last site, and that was what interested her.

"A retail area," she said out loud to Nate. "Stores. Someone locking up and going home for the night."

"It's the same MO for sure," Nate nodded. "It's easy to get them in a place like this when everyone has gone home for the night. Plus it's easy to scope out. You can find out where all the security cameras are and look like you're in the area for legitimate business."

"It's a fantastic place to launch an attack from," Laura agreed glumly. "And unfortunately, there are way too many stores and office sites in this city for us to somehow manage to patrol them all, even with the precinct's help."

"Well, if it was easy, they wouldn't need us," Nate said, flashing her a wry grin.

"Alright," Laura sighed, squaring her shoulders, and trying to convince herself that sitting on top of a bed for a few hours had been enough rest. Nate still thought she'd gone to sleep like he had, and she wasn't going to disabuse him of the notion. He would probably do something annoying like insist she lay her head down while he took over the whole investigation by himself for a few hours. She walked the few steps back to the body, looking down at it. "Similarities – the location has a very similar feel, and we can obviously see that he was strangled using the same weapon or type of weapon as our other two victims."

"He's also lying on his back, which implies he was strangled from behind and dragged down just like they were." Nate leaned down, looking at the ligature marks around their victim's neck from a closer angle. "And just like in those two cases, I'm thinking we're looking for someone with very high levels of strength. I'm not an expert, but I would definitely guess that the expected height and build for this angle would match up to our killer as well. I've got no doubt it was him."

"But, even so," Laura said, taking a breath and gesturing down at the body. "Differences: most obvious – this victim is a man, and the previous two were women."

"And it looks like he fought more," Nate said. "There's a little variation in the ligature marks. Almost just a wobble – but it's there. With the red marks on the ends of his fingertips, I'm guessing that the coroner is going to tell us that he almost managed to fight the killer off. With the cord or whatever you want to call it around his neck, though, he probably had no chance."

"I think you're right," Laura said. She glanced up at Cortez, who was hovering nearby almost nervously. "Security cameras?"

"I have my detectives going door to door for witnesses and cameras now," Cortez said.

"Our witness?"

"It was actually a security officer patrolling the area," Cortez said. She gestured off to the side, towards the parked police cars; Laura assumed he'd been placed inside one of them to ward off the cold air and the shock. "I spoke to him as soon as I arrived. He didn't report seeing anyone in the area, and the body wasn't touched or moved. He'd only just arrived for his first patrol of the night, so he didn't notice anyone hanging around recently. Did you want to speak with him?"

Laura considered it, but shook her head. Cortez seemed to have done a thorough job with her interview. "No, let him go. Wait – ask him if he knows of anyone who was sneaking around over the last month or so, then let him go."

Cortez nodded smartly and stepped away to do as she had been ordered, which left Laura and Nate conveniently alone next to the body. Laura glanced down at the only silent witness to their conversation and then up at the officers guarding the tape, far enough away not to hear them.

"I saw this," she said.

Nate looked at her immediately, his body going taut, on high alert. "You had a vision?"

Laura nodded. "Last night. I was looking through the case files." She avoided looking at him, guilty to be caught out doing work when she told him she was going to rest. "I touched one of the crime scene photographs and then I saw it. This man being yanked backwards with a ligature around his neck, his face going purple."

"Jesus." Nate glanced around, clearly trying to keep his expression neutral as he made sure no one was listening, just like Laura had. "Did you see who did it?"

"No." Laura clenched her hand into a fist momentarily. "I couldn't see him properly. I kept wanting to look over the victim's shoulder, but – it just didn't happen. I saw enough to know it was him, and that's it."

"You watched him die." Nate took a beat, the reached out and put his hand on her shoulder. "I'm sorry."

Laura looked at him with a spark of wry amusement. "You're sorry?"

"You had to watch him die," Nate said. "That must have been awful."

Laura glanced away. "I'm kind of used to it."

Of course, it wasn't totally true. No matter how many deaths she saw, there were still those that affected her the worst. The ones that she felt she should have prevented. Harm coming to people she actually knew or had met. Children.

Children were always the worst.

"Still," Nate said. "I guess it's only just hitting me now that you have to keep watching that happen over and over again. I only have to see the bodies, and that's enough."

"Yeah, well." Laura cleared her throat. "It's our job, isn't it? Anyway, there was more."

"More?" Nate winced.

"I saw him die twice," Laura said. She glanced around again and then stepped closer to Nate so she could lower her voice, well aware that what she was about to say could make her sound insane. "Two visions."

"How is that possible?" Nate asked. "Two different possibilities?"

"No," Laura said, then shook her head. "Or, I don't know. I have no idea why I saw two. But they were really different. It's not like, one time the killer got him here and another time he got him nearer to his house. The other death was a car crash."

"Tonight?" Nate asked with a frown.

Laura hadn't even thought about the timeframe. "I don't know," she admitted. "I didn't have any way to know when it was in the vision. I just saw the crash – I was inside the car. I've never seen anything like that before. One vision and then another right on the heels of it, and both of the same person."

"Huh." Nate seemed to consider it for a minute, then shrugged his shoulders. "I guess we keep investigating and see what comes up. Maybe we'll figure out a way to explain it."

"Yeah, maybe." Laura felt uneasy still. She felt like things were upside down. She was supposed to use her visions to solve crimes. She wasn't supposed to need to look at crimes to solve her visions.

"He didn't see anyone sneaking or hanging around," Sergeant Cortez said, causing Laura to whip around and face the approaching officer. She was coming up to them fast, which reassured Laura that she hadn't heard anything up to that point. "He said there was nothing unusual about the last few months. He only started working at this site a few months back, so he couldn't say about earlier."

"Alright," Laura nodded. "Well, our next step is going to be having a chat with the victim's family. Have we got a successful ID?"

Cortez nodded. "His wallet had a driver's license with his image on it in the name of Haydn Townsend," she said. "We've notified his family, but they aren't here yet. They're out of state. They said they would travel down to formally identify the body, help with the investigation, and start the process of wrapping up his estate, but they won't be here until later today."

"Anyone else we can talk to in the meantime?" Laura asked. "A girlfriend? … Boyfriend?"

"I haven't got any identified significant others just yet, but he does have an employee at his store who seems to have been there for years," Cortez said. "Terry Rush. Do you want me to take you to his residence? He hasn't been informed yet."

"Yes, I do," Laura said, turning back towards their parked car with determination.

They had to do something. She couldn't let it happen like this – for the killer to just keep striking as often as he liked and for them to be asleep on the job.

They were going to catch him. Maybe there was a chance this coworker had the information that would allow them to do it.

Laura wasn't going to waste a single moment in getting to it.

CHAPTER THIRTEEN

Laura wasn't sure whether he was about to throw up or start crying.

She took the seat opposite Terry Rush, taking in just how upset he seemed. Nate dropped onto the sofa beside her. "How long had you been working with Haydn Townsend?" she asked.

Terry blinked, as if unsure of how to even process the question. "Ah… nearly twenty years, now," he said, a slight movement of his fingers as though he was counting the years. "It's… I can't believe it. I just can't believe it."

"I know this must be a very trying time," Laura said. "You must feel terrible. But I need to ask you some questions, and if you can give us the answers to the best of your ability, it's going to increase the likelihood of us finding out who did this."

"I understand," Terry said, nodding and looking down at his hands. He was leaning forward over his own knees, his hands lightly clasped. His face turned even greener, though he didn't rush off or mention any nausea. "I'll do my best. Haydn was… God, more than a boss. We'd worked together so long, the lines get blurred, you know? He buys… he used to buy my daughter Christmas presents."

"I know you must be struggling to process this, so thank you," Laura said. "The first thing I need to know is whether there is anyone, to your knowledge, who would want to harm Mr. Townsend in any way."

"To my knowledge…" Terry trailed off, thinking, his eyes searching from side to side in his memories. "No. There's no one."

"You've never heard of him having a dispute with a customer or a supplier? Anything in his personal life?"

"No, nothing."

"What about his relationship with his family?" Nate asked. "He lived far away from them."

"Yes, but not because they didn't get along," Terry said. "He never married or had kids – he spent a lot of time focusing on the store. When his sister had a child, she ended up moving to get closer to a good school. They never came back. His parents have both passed."

"So, no issues? Not even resentment that they moved away?" Laura asked. She wasn't exactly sure how his own resentment would lead to his murder, but she at least had to try to figure out all the possibilities here. Once armed with all the information, she could figure out what it meant later.

"No, not at all," Terry shrugged. "Every holiday, he would drive up there to spend it with them. And last summer, the kid – he's a teenager now – came down to work in the store and earn some extra money before college. They were close."

Laura nodded, though she was disappointed. They needed something here. "What about the last few months – have you noticed anyone strange or that you don't recognize hanging around the store? Maybe someone who never bought things, or came in to make multiple small purchases, or just hung around outside and never came in?"

Terry shook his head slowly. "No, I can't think of anything."

"Anyone who came in and asked about Mr. Townsend while he wasn't in the store?"

Terry shrugged. "He was always in the store."

Laura tried not to snap at him. It wasn't his fault. There probably hadn't been anything to notice. All three victims so far had apparently not been aware of anyone with murderous intentions towards them. Either these were random attacks based on opportunity, or the killer was very good at not being noticed.

"Alright," she said. A thought occurred to her, and she decided to try to find out what she could about the other vision she'd seen – the one that hadn't come true. "You said he used to drive over to visit family? He was walking home when he was attacked."

"He lived not far from the store," Terry said. "He didn't need the car for work."

"It'll be parked at his home, then," Laura said, she tried to make it sound as though she was thinking out loud, but really she wanted him to confirm it.

"I guess so," Terry shrugged.

"Do you know if he was planning on visiting family or going out of town any time soon?" Laura asked.

Terry shook his head. "He just got back from Christmas not too long ago. He wouldn't have been planning another visit for a while yet. He doesn't like taking time away from the store, so he – I mean, he didn't like…"

"It's alright," Laura said soothingly, seeing how his mood dropped at the sudden re-realization that his boss was dead. She was running out of ways to ask. It wasn't like she could put it all out in the open. *I saw your boss dying in a car crash before I saw him dying from strangulation. I get these psychic visions, see. What do you think it means?*

"Well, if you do think of anything that might be relevant, please get in touch right away," Nate said. "It might not seem obvious to you now – and there might be something you haven't thought of so far because you're in shock. But no matter how small it is, we'll want to know."

"I will," Terry said. He looked miserable. "I really wish I could help."

"What you've given us already may well help," Laura said, trying to make both of them feel better. "We just have to apply it and see what comes up. At any rate – it's the middle of the night, so I'm sure you'll want to get back to your rest."

"Why?" he asked morosely. "It's not like I have to get up for work in the morning now."

"Even so," Laura said. "We'll leave you to it. You may want to call someone to be with, yourself."

Terry nodded distantly, though Laura couldn't even be sure he'd heard her. She got up with Nate right behind her and headed for the door, casting one look back over her shoulder. Terry looked inconsolable, and he hadn't even been able to give them any answers.

"I don't get it," Laura said, as they moved out of earshot and closed the front door behind them. "I had two visions, and nothing I'm hearing explains them. Why would I see him getting into a car crash at the same time as being strangled?"

"I don't know," Nate said. They walked back to the car together slowly. "What does your gut tell you? What would be your first thought about having two conflicting visions?"

"That I was seeing two alternate futures," Laura said. "But I don't… I mean, what is that? Am I supposed to think that if I had been able to save him from the killer, he would have died in a car crash anyway? Is that supposed to be comforting?"

"I don't know if your visions are supposed to do or be anything," Nate said. He opened the passenger side door but leaned on the side of the car for a moment, still talking in the quiet of the dark suburban street. His voice was low, enough that Laura wasn't worried about some local resident overhearing them from the nearby houses. "Aren't they just… there?"

"I don't know," Laura replied, because that was an entirely depressing thought. It was somehow comforting to imagine that she might have some kind of purpose. That something or someone had given her the visions to help her solve crimes. If there was no rhyme or reason behind them at all, that was somehow much worse.

"Well, maybe there's another way of looking at it," Nate said. "Maybe it's not alternate futures. Maybe it's… I don't know, alternate people. Didn't we have that case with the twins before?"

Laura blinked.

How had she not thought of that?

"The twins," she muttered, getting into the car. There was a slam from the other side of the vehicle as Nate did the same and closed his door after him. Of course, the case with the twins had been before Nate knew about her visions. She hadn't been able to tell him about them back then, but she'd had that same confusion. A vision of a person dying in a different way, when they were already dead. It had taken her a while to figure it out then, too.

"Was that similar?" Nate asked. "I didn't know anything about it, so I don't know if that's how it works."

"Kind of," Laura said, nodding. Maybe they were onto something here. "But Terry only mentioned a sister – we need to check his family, see if there's someone else who would fit the bill of sharing his physical characteristics."

"Then let's do that," Nate said. He grabbed his cell phone out of his pocket, twisting his hips to be able to get to it in the car seat, and started dialing. Laura left the car's engine switched off, waiting to find out where they needed to go next before she bothered to start driving.

He put the phone to his ear and there was a moment's pause, then he spoke again. "Ah, Detective Judd," he said, putting the phone on speaker and then setting it in the central console of the car so they could both hear it equally. "We need you to make a few checks on our latest victim. Are you near a computer?"

"Yeah, I'm at my desk," Detective Judd answered. By his voice, Laura identified him as the one she'd dubbed Cool Detective. "Shoot."

"Alright, so, was Haydn Townsend a twin? Or did he have a brother at all?"

There was only a brief pause – not long enough for Judd to finish typing, and Laura could still hear his fingers tapping on his keyboard. "Ohhh – are you thinking this is connected to Ronan Linwood?"

Laura looked at Nate over the phone, glowing between them. "Ronan Linwood?" she repeated.

"Oh, is that Agent Frost?" Judd didn't seem to feel the need to actually wait for an answer. "You guys haven't heard of Linwood? He was big news around here about ten years ago."

Laura frowned. Ten years? How was this relevant? Judd needed to start talking or she was going to get impatient. "Who was he?" she asked.

There was the sound of Judd pausing his typing, turning as if he was picking up the phone to hold it closer to his face and tell the story properly. "He was a total psycho. He was going around the state attacking twins. There was no explanation for it other than complete psychotic paranoia. He just had this thing in his head that twins were evil, or something, so anytime he saw a pair of them he would lose it. He started beating them up and then by the time he was caught, he'd taken to carrying a pocket knife. The last victim got stabbed."

"Which prison is he in?" Nate asked.

"Oh, no, he's not in prison," Judd said. He had the tone of someone who knew he was telling an excellent and shocking story, and also telling it well. "He's out on the streets. That's why he came to mind right away. He got out recently. I don't have anything on the system about any brother, by the way – we'll have to request the information from another agency to find out if he has a twin with no criminal record."

"He served ten years for murder?" Laura asked, unable to believe what she was hearing.

"No one actually died," Judd replied. "The stabbing was non-fatal. He was found guilty of assault but sentenced to serve his time in a hospital. Apparently, he was given a clean bill of mental health recently."

"And released," Laura said, making the assumption but feeling fairly secure in it given the conversation's path this far.

"I can get you the address of the halfway house he's been put into," Judd supplied helpfully.

"That would be great – send it to me as a text," Nate said. "We'd better go and speak to him, if nothing else."

"Thanks, Detective," Laura said, reaching out to end the call. Nate grabbed his phone back and then waited a second, staring at the screen before the text came through.

"Put it in the GPS," Laura said, putting her seatbelt on and reaching to start the engine. It wasn't often a lead this strong came along, fitting exactly with what she had seen in her visions and delivered to them on a plate. "We'd better get over there and see if he came in late. If we're lucky, he might still be wearing the same clothes and we'll nail him on the forensics."

CHAPTER FOURTEEN

Laura turned off the engine and squinted up at the building they had parked out front of, making out two windows full of light on this side and what looked like one more around the other side. "Someone's up," she commented to Nate. It was two in the morning. Why would you be up if not because you'd just been out committing a crime?

"Are we just going straight in?" Nate asked.

"I think we'd better," Laura replied. "There's no time for being clever tonight. If we're right, any second of delay could give him more of a chance to get rid of the evidence. We get in there, arrest him, and get him back to the precinct before he can finish cleaning up."

Nate didn't say anything, as he was reaching for his door and getting out of the car – a tacit agreement that getting on with it right away was the best policy. Laura followed him to the entrance of the building: it looked like a normal residential home, if a large one, but they both knew there was more to it than met the eye. This was a place where criminals leaving institutions or prisons came to stay, to help them acclimate to the real world again. The people who lived here did so temporarily, and each one of them had once been an offender.

Even if they were supposedly reformed, Laura wasn't going to leave an inch of caution outside. They needed to be on their guard here. There was no way to know how the residents would react to waking up and finding a couple of FBI agents in their midst.

Nate knocked loudly; there was only a short pause before the door opened, which was unusual enough in itself. It was the middle of the night, after all.

But even more unexpected was the fact that the man opening the door was, judging by the quick web search Nate had conducted on the way over, exactly who they were looking for.

"Ronan Linwood?" Laura asked, almost too shocked to find her voice for a minute.

"Yes?" he said, looking between them. If he was alarmed to be visited at this time of the night by people who were obviously law enforcement, he didn't say it.

"I'm Special Agent Frost, with Special Agent Lavoie," Laura said. "We need to talk with you."

"Okay," he said, stepping aside, just like that. "Please, come in."

Laura almost stumbled at how easy it was to get him to comply so far. Was this him trying to play the system, to see if he could trick them into leaving by appearing unworried? Most ex-cons, whether they had been to prison or to a mental health institution, were going to be wary around cops. It didn't matter what kind of subterfuge he tried to pull. They were going to do a full and thorough investigation, no matter what. Being invited in meant that they could look around without a warrant, so that was the first step.

Laura followed him without comment; he led them through a narrow corridor to a large room at the back of the house, which appeared to be a kitchen and living space all rolled into one. It was big enough for perhaps even ten people to use the space at once, which was evidently useful in a place like this. He gestured towards a large battered-looking sofa and several armchairs and then towards the kitchen.

"Please, take a seat," he said. "Would you like a coffee? Tea?"

"No, thank you," Laura said. Coffee at this time of night was tempting, given the lack of sleep, but then again she wasn't convinced she wanted to sample a drink in this kind of place served to her by a potential murderer. She glanced at Nate.

"Why don't you take a seat?" he asked. "We can get comfortable and ask our questions without having to feel so formal. I'm going to find your bathroom real quick."

"First door on the left at the top of the stairs," Ronan said, without taking his eyes off Laura. She felt a shiver run through her but did her best to disguise it. He sat opposite her, shrugging. "I'm an open book. Please, ask whatever you need to know."

"Alright," Laura said. She felt, rather than watched, Nate leave the room. She could trace his footsteps down the hall and then up the stairs. She felt exposed here without him, but one of them had to try to check out their suspect's room and one of them had to distract him. If it was the other way around, she would have been feeling her heart pound, jumping at every shadow, hoping one of the other residents wasn't waiting behind a door with a knife – or a garotte. "Mr. Linwood, you were recently released from a correctional facility – a hospital, isn't that correct?"

"Yes." He inclined his head. "I was there for nine years and seven months. After I committed my violent crimes, I was diagnosed with untreated schizophrenia. I was having delusions and hallucinations related to the idea that twins were a sign of evil, and that they wanted to do great harm to me. After receiving treatment, I no longer suffer from the same delusions, so they deemed me fit for release."

"Did you feel fit for release?" Laura asked.

Linwood looked down at the floor for a moment. "Sometimes, no," he admitted. "I know I'm better now, but what I did haunts me. It's not like I was blacked out or I didn't know what I was doing – I remember all of it. I remember them crying out in pain, begging me to stop, trying to protect one another. I carry profound guilt now for what I did to my victims. I feel sometimes like I should be locked away to rot forever for that."

"Did you ask to stay in the facility?" Laura pressed. She was building some idea in her head now. A man who wanted so badly to be punished that he would do anything to go back inside again. Did that fit with what she saw in front of her now? Or was it too much of a notion that he would go and create more guilt for himself, if he suffered with it so badly?

"I didn't," Linwood shrugged. "I could have, I suppose, but I don't think it would have made much difference. I had a lot of talks with my therapist about what this would mean – being in the outside world again. Apparently, it's really common for people to have anxiety and fears about coming out. Rather than a reason to stay locked up, it's something to be medicated and worked through. That's what I'm working on in my weekly sessions now."

"You're still going to regular therapy?" At his nod, Laura continued. "What do you feel about twins now?"

Linwood broke into a half-smile and shook his head. "It's the weirdest thing. I don't feel anything. Apart from the guilt. Seeing twins now just reminds me that I hurt some twins in the past – but I don't see any of the delusions I used to have anymore. They're just... people. Like anyone else."

Laura was beginning to feel frustrated with his entirely reasonable answers. He wasn't giving her anything to work on. He seemed so polite, so sincere, so reformed. She was going to have to go in harder to get him to slip up. "Have you been following the latest local murders in the news?"

"There are always murders around here," Linwood sighed. "Which ones?"

"The strangulations," Laura said. "You may have seen the first one reported on heavily – Brooke Ware. She was a beautiful young woman."

"Oh, yes," Linwood said, brightening a little. Laura couldn't tell if it was because he was pleased to know the answers to what she was talking about, or whether he enjoyed this murder in particular. "I did read about that. It's terrible. And there was another one a couple of days ago, wasn't there? Another woman."

"A therapist," Laura said evenly. She wasn't going to come out and accuse him yet, but she wanted him to feel the growing pressure. The links to him. Violence, criminality in the local area, the fact that he was familiar with therapists himself.

"That's so sad," he said, shaking his head. "People that help others like that – we should be protecting them above anyone else."

There was a soft thump from above. Laura's eyes shot skywards for a moment. She really hoped that was Nate accidentally knocking something over, not Nate getting stabbed and falling to the floor. "I agree," Laura said. "It's a shame. But I would really prefer a world where no one was murdered at all, regardless of their job."

"Oh, of course," Linwood said. "You're right. I guess it's hard to stop human nature. I wish that wasn't part of it, but it is. I just hope that you're able to catch whoever did it quickly and give them the treatment they need so no one else gets hurt."

"Me, too," Laura said, wondering if they were both talking about him. "Mr. Linwood, why are you up so late?"

"I just got in," Linwood said casually. He reached for a cup of coffee on the table and sipped at it, clearly having been drinking it already before she knocked on the door.

Laura blinked. Was that an admission?

"Where have you been?" she asked, which she felt was obviously part of the original question anyway.

"At work," Linwood said, setting his coffee cup down and looking back at her evenly.

"Work?" Laura repeated. A horrible feeling was beginning to dawn on her.

Linwood had been so polite. Welcomed them inside without any objection at all. He'd answered all their questions and spoken about how his mental health problems were now under control.

And now…

He had an alibi?

"Yes," Linwood said. "I work at one of the factories on the west side of town. It makes toothpicks, of all things. Most of the work is done by robots now, but they need someone there at all times to supervise them and do quality checks. I couldn't get work anywhere else, and they didn't really want me on shift with all the others in the day, but they gave me the late evening shift."

"How long have you been working at the factory?" Laura asked. Her mouth was dry. She had a feeling she knew the answer already.

"A couple of months now," Linwood said. "The guy who runs this place, Jeff, he got me the job as soon as I was out. He said it was good to go into an environment with rules and schedules like in prison, you know? Helps make the transition easier. I mean, I was in hospital, not prison, but it's a similar situation, I guess."

Laura nodded. "And you work five days a week?"

"Seven, actually," Linwood said. He gave her a wry grin. "It's a shorter shift, so perfectly legal. And it's not like I have this busy social life for the work to interfere with. It gives me something to do, honestly."

"How many days of work have you missed since starting?" Laura asked.

"None."

Laura took a deep breath. This was a waste of time. They were barking up the wrong tree – vision or no vision. The whole thing had been a wild goose chase.

Nate chose that precise moment to come back down the stairs and give her a minute shake of his head, indicating that he'd found nothing suspicious up there either.

"Did you know Brooke Ware, Jessika Granger, or Haydn Townsend?" Laura asked. It was the last thing she could think of. A last-ditch attempt to find some kind of connection between them.

"I've only heard of the first one," Linwood replied. "And only from the news reports even then. I don't know the other two. Who are they?"

"No one," Laura replied, more to get his attention away from them and avoid answering the question than out of dismissiveness for their lives. She stood up, nodding at Nate to indicate that they were done here. "We've taken enough of your time, Mr. Linwood. Thank you for answering my questions."

"Not a problem," Linwood said. And then, with perceptive gentleness, he added: "And I can give you my supervisor's number if you want to check out my alibi and get their security footage."

Laura looked at him for a moment, but he wasn't an idiot. Anyone would have been able to guess why two FBI agents would come and interview a previously violent offender during the middle of a publicized murder spree.

"Thanks," Laura nodded again, and then led Nate out into the cold air of the night.

She managed to hold herself back until they were both inside the car – and then she let out a frustrated groan, throwing her head back against the seat.

"Okay, it didn't work out," Nate said. "But we have to pursue every lead, right?"

"Please don't be reasonable right now," Laura moaned, shaking her head. "I can't take it."

Nate chuckled, and in spite of herself, Laura felt her spirit lift just a bare inch at the sound.

"Where are we now?" Nate asked. "We don't have any suspects left."

"We need to speak to Townsend's family and see if they can shed any light on everything," Laura said. "But they're on the way here still. Until we get the call from Cortez, we have to kick our heels on that part."

"Well, then we have two choices," Nate said. "Either we go to the precinct and start poring over everything, going through social media accounts, reviewing all the files, checking the coroner's reports again, and trying to see if there's any small link or clue that we've missed. Or we go back to the motel and get a few more hours' sleep."

Laura thought about it. Sleep was tempting. Especially as Nate didn't even know that she hadn't slept at all earlier.

But this case was getting under her skin, and she didn't want to have to get woken up even one more time and told that someone had died on their watch. She wanted to stop this killer now, before anyone else had to lose their life.

With that in mind, the choice was easy.

"Let's head over to the precinct," she said. "We can get as much work done as possible before the family get here. They said it's only a couple of hours, right?"

"Right," Nate said. And Laura started the engine, ready to drive away.

CHAPTER FIFTEEN

Laura stopped for a moment outside of the interview room, trying to take a deep breath.

"You alright?" Nate asked.

Laura shrugged and nodded at the same time. "Just a lot, isn't it? Talking to the families."

"It always is," Nate nodded, sighing. "It's part of the job, though, I guess."

"I know that." A spark of annoyance flared through Laura, but she tamped it down. She knew Nate was trying to make her feel better, not patronize her. "I just wish it wasn't. Or that at least we could be talking to people about how their family member survived instead of talking to the bereaved."

"Next one," Nate said. "Don't ever forget about that. For all the families who've lost someone, we always manage to solve the case. Then we don't have to talk to the family of the next one, because we saved them."

That was a brighter way of looking at it, Laura supposed. Still. There were parts of this job she hated.

"Alright, then," she said, gesturing towards the door. It wasn't going to get any easier, no matter how long she stood outside and tried to brace herself. "Let's go in."

The interview room that had been set aside for the family was much more comfortable than those that suspects were normally taken to. This wasn't a stark affair with a table and four chairs around it in front of a one-way window. No, this was a soft sofa, bright primary colors, blankets, and cushions. It was the interview room that was used for talking to child victims or women who had come forward to report assault. Safe, soft, comfortable.

The irony, of course, was that no one was ever really comfortable in this room, given that they were always there to live through the aftermath of a crime.

Laura approached the family softly, not knowing yet how they were going to react. They weren't as close to Townsend as some of the other families she interviewed – people who had lost sons, fathers. But losing a brother and an uncle wasn't something to be sniffed at either.

"Hello," she greeted them, making her way to another soft sofa just opposite the one that the man, woman, and teenager had seated themselves on. "My name is Special Agent Laura Frost. I'm here investigating the string of murders that we believe Mr. Townsend's death is linked to."

"I'm Special Agent Nathaniel Lavoie," Nate said, extending a hand to shake as he sat down beside her. The man, balding and overweight with a moustache from the eighties, was the only one to take it.

"What string of murders?" the woman, who was very clearly Haydn Townsend's sister from the family resemblance, yet with hair dyed a vibrant red on top of it, said. "What's happening here?"

Laura lifted a hand to slow down her questions, nodding sympathetically. "This must be a lot to take in. We had already been called down here because there have been two murders over the last five days. We landed this morning and began to investigate, but I'm afraid it looks as though your brother is the latest victim of the same attacker."

"How did he…?" the sister trailed off. Her face was distraught, and the man and teenage boy didn't look much better. Laura spared a glance for the boy, deciding he had to be over sixteen and that she would therefore leave it to his mother's judgement what he could and couldn't hear.

"He was strangled with a kind of thin plastic wire," Laura said. "That's all we know at this point. I'm afraid we don't have any witnesses. We have security footage of the assailant and we are following leads to track him down, so please rest assured that we are doing absolutely everything we can at this point to find him and stop him from doing this to anyone else."

"Why couldn't you stop him doing it to Uncle Haydn?"

Laura looked at the teenage boy, feeling the bottom drop out of her stomach. He was right. She hadn't helped his uncle. She hadn't stopped the killer from striking again. She'd been on the ground for a whole day and still hadn't made enough progress to protect another victim.

"I'm sorry," she said, looking down at the ground. "I don't think there are any words we could possibly say to ease the pain of his passing for you, but I promise you, we're doing everything we can to stop this. No matter what it takes, we will catch him."

Laura felt Nate shift restlessly beside her and knew that he was uncomfortable with her words. Making a promise like that was usually discouraged. Telling someone that you were going to get a positive result could open you up for litigation – or at the very least, some extremely hurt feelings – if you actually couldn't follow through.

Logically, Laura knew that there were unsolved cases out there. There were serial killers who had taken far more lives than this one so far managed, and yet who were unknown – Zodiac, for example. The net was closing in on those types all the time. The Golden State Killer hadn't evaded justice for his whole life.

But that didn't mean that families wouldn't be left extremely upset and disappointed if Laura ended up having to move on and consign the case to a cold case department instead of solving it within the next few days.

But it didn't matter. The pressure she might feel from them was nothing. She already put enough pressure on her own head, knowing that if she didn't catch him, it was likely that no one could.

"We need to ask you a few questions," Nate said, smoothly taking over to distract from her hasty promise. "I know this is a difficult time and it may be distressing to talk about, but the more information we have, the better chance we have of catching this killer."

"Go ahead," the husband said, nodding vigorously. "We'll do whatever we can."

"First of all, can you think of anyone that might have a grudge against Haydn, want to harm him, or so on, no matter how unreasonable it might seem to you?" Nate asked.

There was a pause as the three family members glanced at each other, shaking their heads. Laura was already getting that sinking feeling that they weren't going to be any help. They hadn't been close enough by to know everything about Townsend's life. If his closest coworker, and likely the person with whom he spent the most time in life, couldn't tell them anything, then what could they expect from these distant relatives?

"When was the last time you spoke to him?" Nate asked. It sounded like he was trying to establish a starting point of how useful they would even be.

"At Christmas," the sister replied promptly. "He came to stay with us and left on New Year's Day."

"And did he mention anything unusual?" Nate asked. "Any weird feelings, any people he didn't like the look of, anyone new in his life at all?"

"No," the sister said. She looked like she, too, was realizing how unhelpful they were being and was upset by it.

"Do you recall Mr. Townsend ever being involved in a car accident?" Laura asked. It probably sounded like an abrupt change of direction for the others, but the question had been brewing inside her for a while. If they couldn't help with the understanding of Haydn Townsend's personal life and circumstances, then maybe they could help shed some light on the vision Laura had – without bringing it up in such a way that she had some awkward explaining to do.

"Yes," the sister replied. "How did you know?"

Laura blinked.

"It was a severe accident?" she asked, needing to know if it matched up with what she had seen. The scattered glass of the windshield. The blood on his face. The flashing lights from the ambulance reflecting off it all.

"Oh, yes, very severe. He barely walked away with his life."

Laura glanced at Nate. She could tell he knew how significant this was. He stayed quiet, letting her control the direction of the questioning. She needed to know more.

"Can you tell me about that?" Laura asked. "In detail, I want to know what happened."

"Uh," she said, her eyes going to the ceiling as she remembered. "Well, I don't know how much I know. Let's see. He was driving home from seeing us a year or two ago. Around this time of year, actually. As he was going across a crossroads, this truck came out of nowhere and T-boned him."

"It was really serious," the husband added, seemingly relieved that he finally had something he could chime in on. "The car ended up upside down. I've seen the photos from the first responders. The whole windshield was blown out, and as he was the only one in the car, he took the brunt of everything. He was unconscious, just kept in place by his seatbelt."

"He always told me to wear my seatbelt because of that," the teenage son said quietly. "I always did after he told me what it was like."

"They had to airlift him to hospital," the sister added. "I remember getting this phone call in the middle of the night to say that we had to get there, fast. We didn't think he was going to make it. But he was so lucky – he just had a broken leg, a concussion, and a scar on his temple in the end. The doctors said they had no idea how he walked away from it – that the EMTs said it was one of the worst crashes they'd ever seen where the person was alive inside. And – oh…"

Something came over the sister's face then, a sudden rush as if she was crumpling in on herself. Laura had the feeling she'd gotten wrapped up in the story, remembering the sensations of it: the relief and the joy that her brother had survived, that this miracle had happened, and he was okay. And then she'd remembered the rest. The fact that he wasn't okay anymore.

"Thank you," Laura said. "That's really helpful."

"Is it?" the husband asked, catching her off guard. Normally, she wouldn't expect family members to be sharp enough at this stage to wonder why she was asking certain questions. "How is that relevant?"

"I'm not sure yet," Laura admitted with a wry smile. "But every bit of the puzzle adds up to something. And this will certainly help us with making a positive identification – though we'll still need your help on that part."

It was a little white lie. Of course, the identification thing was true. But Laura's mind was racing over the information in a different way.

The vision she had seen was now fully explained. What she had seen had been a real event, not something made up or a potential different future. It had been a glimpse of the past. The victim had previously had a near death experience which almost resulted in the loss of his life, though he had managed to survive – only to die now at the hands of the killer.

That was significant – it had to be. Seeing both deaths meant there had to be something to read into them. The first one, which didn't stick, and the second, which did. There was some link between them.

And there was another thought which followed that, too. Nate had been right about them having a case with twins before that had similar visions. But there had been another case which reminded her of this one, now. Another case in which the killer had targeted people he perceived should have died years before. Those who had been saved after their hearts already stopped.

Was this another killer suffering from the same delusion? That people who had near death experiences were breaking the flow of natural life and had to be killed in order to bring things back to the correct order and avoid further evil?

There was only one way she could be sure if the link she had seen was something significant or something worthless. She needed to find out if the other two victims had near death experiences of a similar nature, too.

"If you think of anything that we haven't gone over yet, I'd really like you to call me," she said, taking a business card out of her pocket and passing it over to the sister. "Even if you're not sure that it's relevant – let us be the ones to decide. You'll be kept up to date, too, by the local detectives. I know this is an awful time, so please take some time to process what has happened – are you staying locally?"

"We're going to stay at Haydn's home for a few days," the husband explained.

Laura nodded. For a moment she didn't know if they should stay there and potentially ruin any evidence – but she wasn't even sure what she would be looking for, and the killing had happened near his workplace, not his home. She couldn't justify keeping them from it on the possibility that they might one day maybe need to search the place. "If you happen across anything that looks significant, please give us a call."

"We will," he promised, and Laura took that as her cue to get up.

"Alright," she said, nodding to them. "We'll leave you alone for a short while. Someone will be along in a moment to speak with you about any other arrangements you need."

There was a murmured goodbye from the sofa, from the husband and sister. Laura and Nate walked out of the room, and Laura closed the door behind them softly with barely a click.

"We've got something, haven't we?" Nate asked.

"Yes," Laura said. There was a gleam in her eyes. "And I know exactly what we have to do next."

CHAPTER SIXTEEN

He sat in the parking lot with the lights off, watching silently. He was always watching silently in the dark these days. But it didn't matter. This was part of his life now, he supposed.

The barista was cleaning the tables and putting chairs up on top of them, seats facing down, like she did every night. It was boring, physical work, he thought, but she didn't seem to mind. Maybe that was the difference between them. She could just go on living this mundane life day after day and didn't aspire to anything else.

He'd been watching her for a while and he couldn't see any sign of anything else. Not like he had: the anger, bubbling away just under the surface. It was as though she didn't feel it. But how could that be the case?

Maybe he should have admired her. Even asked her how she did it – how she coped each day without wanting to burn the whole place down. Hearing it from her might have helped him to deal with it himself. Might have taught him how to do it.

But he didn't want to learn.

One day he would. One day, he would have cleared his demons and found a way to carry on. One day he would burn out all the anger and be left with whatever else there was. But not today.

Not until she was dead.

Her, and all the others.

The barista went around behind the counter and started doing something with the register – counting up all the cash that had been paid in that day and reconciling it with the records. It was going to take her a while. He didn't mind that. He'd waited here a few times and watched her do this precise process, and he knew how long it would take. He didn't mind settling in and watching her.

He only had to watch her this time, and then the next time, he would be ready. So long as nothing changed in her routine, so long as she went from the register and then turned off the lights –

And there she went, taking one final look around to check she had done everything she needed to before she flicked the switch.

He checked his watch. Right on time. She'd been working there for long enough that she had closing up down to a fine art. She did everything in the same order and it took her the same amount of time, every time. You could set your watch by her.

Which was good because that was almost exactly what he was going to do.

He watched with hungry eyes as she stepped outside and locked the door with a jingle of a hefty set of keys, then dropped them inside her purse for safety. She walked then with a brisk step towards the parking lot, towards exactly where he was sitting. He knew he couldn't be seen. He had deliberately set it up like that: He'd parked his car alongside her workplace and then moved into the back seat, where the tinted glass would make it impossible for her to make him out in the darkness. But he could still see her. He watched her walk to her car, parked conveniently close at the edge of the parking lot. That was going to be the one challenge. Making sure he got to her before she reached safety, without giving her the chance to run.

He wasn't particularly worried about it.

She sat inside her car, started the engine, and drove away. After a moment he got out of the car and walked around to the driver's seat, getting in to follow her. He didn't really need to know where she went or what she did next. It wasn't relevant to his plans. But just in case – in case she slipped out of his grasp and he needed another chance – he followed. She drove home, parked, and went inside. He couldn't see much of an opportunity there.

It had to be the parking lot.

And next time he saw her, that was exactly where they were both going to be.

CHAPTER SEVENTEEN

Laura rubbed her eyes with her hands, trying to clear them. She had that kind of dry feeling of having been awake for far too long. It didn't matter. She took another sip of her coffee, then a larger gulp, figuring she might need several cups to make a difference.

She looked down and checked the time on her cell phone – nearly five in the morning. She couldn't help but notice as she did so that there were no messages or missed call notifications on her screen. Nothing from Chris, still.

She was beginning to feel like there was never going to be anything from Chris.

"I think I reached the bottom of the subject," Nate said, sighing and rubbing his own face. He was sitting opposite her, both of them using computers that sat on adjacent desks. "I'm not getting anything new."

"So, seeing a light at the end of a tunnel, flashbacks of your life, high points and low points, talking to people in heaven – that's kind of the whole story?" Laura said.

"And the out of body experiences," Nate said. "Don't forget that."

"Right, how could I?" Laura sighed. It all seemed so... stupid. She'd never seen anything like that when she'd come close to death – and she'd faced off against serial killers who were determined to make sure she never went home. Maybe she just hadn't come close enough yet.

"Afterwards, it's a bleaker picture. PTSD, anxiety, depression, survivor's guilt. Do you think that might be a factor here? Some kind of guilt?"

"Maybe." Laura shrugged and shook her head. "I don't know. I feel like we've spent hours researching this and all we have are the same old clichés you always see on TV. I don't even know whether people really experience these things, or whether they just think they do because it's what they're expecting."

"I know what you mean," Nate said. "And what I'm struggling to understand is how we can use this. Okay, so we know a lot about the way people with near death experiences feel them. We know about how

92

they can disrupt lives. We just don't know what that has to do with our killer. Or the other two victims, for that matter."

"Yeah, well, we're getting closer to that last part, at least," Laura said, checking the time again. Not long before they could reasonably go wake up the families of the victims and speak to them. "Although – oh, my God."

"What?" Nate asked, instantly on high alert.

"It must be sleep deprivation. That's the only way to explain it. I'm just so tired, I'm not thinking straight."

"What?" Nate demanded again, putting his hands flat on the desk in an expression of exasperation.

"Jessika Granger – she was working with patients who had PTSD from near death experiences," Laura said. "That's the link. She worked with patients who had one, and Haydn Townsend had one, too."

"Right!" Nate snapped his fingers. "Damnit. I'm going to blame the sleep deprivation too. We just kind of ruled out the patient connection to the extent that I forgot about the possibility."

"Maybe this is it," Laura said. "Maybe the killer is one of her patients and that's how he knows Haydn Townsend."

"But Townsend wasn't in Jessika's patient files," Nate frowned.

"Right. Oh!" Laura's head shot up. "Maybe she had someone who used to be a patient but moved on to a different therapist. Or she refused to see them because they had violent tendencies. That might make them mad enough to include her on their kill list, right? And the killer could have met Townsend through this other therapist. Or maybe some kind of support group."

Nate cocked his head to one side. "Laura... how many coffees have you had tonight?"

Laura cleared her throat. "That has nothing to do with anything."

Nate chuckled. "Alright, we're making a lot of leaps here, so let's start with looking at local stories about near death experiences and see if there's anyone who stands out."

"Um."

Laura glanced up. One of Cortez's team – Overweight Detective – had been hovering at a nearby desk all night, apparently doing paperwork until he was needed. He was watching them both now with a nervous expression on his face.

"What is it?" Nate asked.

"Well, I just overheard you talking about people who stood out with regards to near death experiences," he said. "And well, someone does come to mind."

"Who?" Laura asked eagerly. She had a good feeling about this line of inquiry.

"There was a local guy who got brought in a few years ago," he said. He scratched the back of his head. "I only remember it because it was so weird. He was harassing people and a couple of them got together to make a complaint. There was nothing that really came out of it – he wasn't doing anything illegal. We just advised him to stop and that was the last I heard of it."

"Tell us more," Laura said, turning toward him fully. From the way he recoiled just slightly, she had a feeling that Nate was right: maybe she'd had too much coffee.

"Okay, well, his name was Pace or something. I remember that, too, because – well, again, it's a weird name. I can look up the notes for you if you want?"

"You have notes?" Laura asked. "I thought you said nothing came of it? Just a complaint?"

"Yeah, but I kept my own notes," he said. "Hold on." He moved back to his desk, clicking around a few times on his screen. He started to type into a search bar, maddeningly slow; even from the next desk over, Laura could make out him typing, one-fingered, P-A-C-E.

"Alright," he said. "Yeah, I have it here. Pace Christinsin," Overweight Detective said. "He was going around calling himself the Death Guru."

"The Death Guru?" Nate repeated, giving Laura significant look.

"Yeah, he said he was an expert in death, whatever that means," the detective said, reading off the screen. "I think he had social media pages under that name. So, when these two people came in to make the complaint, it was about them having had near death experiences. They said he wouldn't leave them alone – he was always asking them about what they'd gone through and trying to get more and more details about it. They were both pretty upset. They were recovering from what had happened, and all that."

"I can imagine," Laura nodded. "Did they mention what he was interested in, in particular? And what kind of vibe he had – curious, angry, violent?"

"He was just really intense," the detective said. "My notes say he kept asking over and over again what they saw in the moment right before they almost died – right before they were saved."

Laura looked at Nate. "What if he's doing this so he can observe what happens in that moment? Or if he's trying to get them to tell him what they see, but he keeps going too far and pushing them right over the edge?"

Nate nodded. "That's a good working theory."

"Do you have an address for this Pace Christinsin?" Laura asked, turning back to their detective.

"Sure," he said, rolling his chair around back to his computer again and starting to type. "I'll get it for you now."

"Great," Laura said, standing up. "It's getting on towards dawn. I think it's time we paid him a visit."

"Agreed," Nate nodded, grabbing the car keys from where they lay on the desk. "I'll drive."

***

Laura hesitated before knocking on the door, eyeing the sign that had been placed on it. It was very clearly a custom job, something made specifically for the owner of this home. It read, *KNOCK FOR THE DEATH GURU.*

As if anyone standing on the doormat – cheerfully themed with a waving skeleton – was going to need instructions for how to get someone to come to the door.

She knocked, holding her breath, and was rewarded by a sound coming from somewhere upstairs in the home. Given that the residents were probably sleeping, she waited, not knocking again but instead giving them time to get down to the door.

It opened with a wrench a few moments later, revealing a man who was hastily drawing a gown closed over what looked like very innocuous pajamas. He was tall and gaunt, with sunken cheeks and a mess of dark hair over his eyes. "Hello?"

Laura lifted her badge to show him. "Special Agent Laura Frost and my partner, Special Agent Nathaniel Lavoie. May we come inside?"

"Uh, sure," he said, stepping back and gesturing. He self-consciously ran a hand back through his hair, which did nothing at all to neaten it. "Just take a seat through there."

Laura followed his directions and stepped through into a room that was certainly death themed. There were skeletons of all kinds of small animals inside bell jars and display cases, different types of skull-themed artwork on the walls, and everything was either painted or upholstered in black. There was a click as Christinsin turned a light on, but the bulb was a dim glow only, leaving it still not so easy to see what was going on in the space.

"You're Pace Christinsin, yes?" she asked, pausing in the middle of the room to look back at him. "Or are we supposed to call you the Death Guru?"

A somewhat pleased expression came over his face. "That's me, yes," he said. "Are you here for a consultation?"

"A consultation?" Laura asked, taking a seat on a black velvet sofa. Nate remained by the door, ostensibly looking at some framed black and white photographs of what appeared to be Victorians – though Laura knew he was actually blocking the exit.

Christinsin sat down in his own armchair, crossing his legs comfortably. He was obviously not used to greeting people in pajamas and a robe, but in this room in his own domain, he seemed to be settling into it easily. "I provide a number of services," he said. "As an expert in death, since you're here to investigate the murders, I guess you need my help."

"Something like that," Laura said smoothly. There was no point in disavowing him of the notion right now. He would soon figure it out for himself. "Did you know any of the victims?"

He tilted his head to one side. "I only know the name of the first one for sure – Brooke Ware," he said. "The second one was named locally in the press as Jessika Granger, but I don't know if that has been confirmed."

"Those are correct," Laura said. "And there's the third – Haydn Townsend."

Christinsin's eyebrows shot up. "A third?" he said. "My, my. Someone has been busy. No, I don't know any of these individuals."

"Are you sure about that?" Laura asked, watching him closely.

"Yes, quite sure," he said. "Why? Should I?"

"I'm surprised," Laura said. She kept her tone casual, as if she were discussing the weather, but she was carefully gauging his reaction. "I would have thought you would be aware of them, given the connection to near death experiences they have."

96

Christinsin sat upright in his chair. "There's a connection? What is it?"

Laura ignored that question. "Are you sure you haven't spoken to any of them before? Not even, perhaps, interviewed Haydn Townsend? We know from records that you're interested in that kind of experience."

"I haven't interviewed him." Christinsin shook his head in what seemed to be wonder. "What a shame! I had no idea there was someone else local that I could have spoken to. Now, what a waste. He'll take that whole experience to his grave. I so wanted to know about it – I love to talk to anyone I can that has been through that kind of thing."

"What's it all in aid of?" Laura asked, trying to sound conversational. "I mean, why are you so interested in the topic?"

"I'm interested in the secrets that they can tell me," he said. "You see, I believe it's all part of a larger puzzle. That when we're about to die, we get just a small glimpse of what lies beyond. A tiny one – so small that we can't even comprehend what we've seen. But if we add all the glimpses that everyone has together, we can start to see a larger part of the picture. It's my strong belief that if we get enough little glimpses, enough witness statements, then we'll be able to know what the afterlife is really like. And even if there is one, since I know there are those who have their doubts."

Laura nodded as if this was all fascinating. "I see," she said. "And are interviews the only way to get those kinds of reports? That information?"

"Well, no, I suppose there are other ways," Christinsin shrugged. "One excellent way to do it is to experience it for yourself. There's nothing like experiencing something yourself to help you understand it – with this kind of mystical event, there's always something lost in translation when you try to tell the story to someone else. And, of course, there are accounts all over the internet. People who share their stories with the world so I don't have to go looking and interview them."

"How about seeing it happen to someone else close up?" Laura asked.

Christinsin looked at her in some surprise. "I don't know. I suppose you might learn something from that if they're able to communicate with you, though most of the time people aren't if they're going through a near death experience."

"So you wouldn't be tempted to give it a try?" Laura asked.

"You know, perhaps I should give it a try," he said, and the sinister tone in his voice made Laura's hairs stand up on the back of her neck. "I'd have to find a way to witness people just as they were dying. What do you think? How might I be able to do that?"

"I would say strangling them to death might be a good way," Laura replied, her voice low.

Christinsin looked at her. It was as though he had seen only what he wanted to see, before – but now he was really looking at her.

"I don't know if I should answer any more of your questions," he said.

"Well, I thought you might say that," Laura said. "That's why I thought we might continue this conversation at the precinct. If you'll give us your full cooperation, I'm sure it won't take long to clear everything up."

"I would like to speak to a lawyer," Christinsin said, a rapid leap from his schmoozy assumption they were here for his help to completely clamming up. "I'm not speaking to you any further until I have a lawyer sitting next to me."

"I think you'll want to talk to us," Nate said. He was still hulking in the doorway, filling the frame with his own.

"Is that a threat?" Christinsin asked, leaping to his feet.

"No, it's a statement of facts," Nate said. "We're just talking for now. This isn't a formal interview. But we could make it one, if you wanted. We could head down to the precinct."

"Screw this," Christinsin muttered hastily, and charged – right at Nate.

Laura only had enough time to leap to her own feet, her hand going to her gun, before the two men collided. Nate closed the gap between him and the doorframe by turning to stand fully on towards Christinsin, right as Christinsin flew into him, attempting to get by. Laura heard and almost felt the impact herself: a thud and crunch of Christinsin's much lighter body hitting Nate's and finding it an immovable object.

"Where do you think you're trying to go?" Nate asked, struggling with the other man. He may have been wiry, especially compared to Nate's muscular build, but he was almost getting away – twisting and turning and attempting to duck past Nate. The only problem he faced was that there wasn't actually any room for him to get past at all.

"Hey!" Laura shouted, trying to stun him with the loud noise so that he would stay still for a minute. "That's enough!" She moved closer, close enough to reach out and grab Christinsin's arm – but he threw her off, almost sending her flying backwards but for her excellent balance.

"Alright," Nate said, in his not-playing-any-more tone, and managed to push and twist Christinsin swiftly until he had one of his arms pulled up against his own back. Christinsin gasped in pain, tapping on his own leg to indicate he'd had enough, and Laura recovered to snap a handcuff on the wrist that was in the air.

She and Nate worked together: He brought Christinsin's arm down and she caught the other to cuff it quickly into place before their suspect could wriggle away. Once restrained, he huffed for breath, and Laura saw him glare at her over his shoulder.

"I want a lawyer," he repeated.

"And you'll get one," Nate promised. "For now, I'm arresting you for assault on an FBI agent. We'll go from there, shall we?"

***

Laura paced up and down in front of the black glass, watching Christinsin and his annoying smug face and wishing she could do something about it.

"I'm sure it won't be long now," Nate said. He was almost placid about it.

"How can you be so calm?" Laura asked. "We've been waiting an hour for this damn lawyer already!"

Nate shrugged. "I guess I'm just glad we have him in custody. Even if the lawyer helps him weasel out of a confession, we've got the assault charge in place. We can hold him until that's been processed and we'll have more time to get our case together and make it stick."

"Then we should be doing something now instead of just waiting," Laura said. "We ought to go back to our desks. We could -"

A knock at the door cut her off.

"Yes?" she called out.

Sergeant Cortez opened the door and peered around it. "Hi. I just thought you'd like to know – the lawyer is here."

"Great," Laura said, walking outside with a gesture that was half relief and half unbridled frustration. "Then let's get him in there and talking to his client so we can get on with this interview. Where are we with anything else?"

Cortez glanced down the hall as a man in a slick suit with a suitcase waltzed toward them in the company of one of the detectives. Laura didn't need to be an FBI agent or have psychic visions to figure out that this was the long-awaited lawyer. He fixed the three of them with a grin that flashed white teeth, stopping only just short of winking at them, before heading into the interview room. Laura tried not to seethe too hard.

"We have the initial reports back from forensics and the coroner for Haydn Townsend," Cortez said, with the lawyer now out of earshot. "Unfortunately, it's nothing new. Almost everything matches up with the other two cases, and there's nothing of evidentiary value."

"Great." Laura sighed. "Door to door witness search and security footage?"

"Nothing this time." Cortez tried to brighten a little, but the effort it took undermined the effect. "We weren't able to reach everyone so late last night, so we've got more patrols going around this morning. We might be able to get a result, still."

"Keep us posted," Laura said, narrowly managing to refrain from growling. She turned and then found herself tapping her foot, realizing there was nowhere to go.

"I really think you should cut down on the coffee," Nate remarked, watching the figure of Sergeant Cortez move away from them back down the hall.

"I need it," Laura snapped, harder than she intended to. She took a deep breath to calm herself before continuing. "I'm tired. If I don't drink the coffee, I won't be able to work properly."

"I'm not saying to stop drinking it entirely," Nate said reasonably. How could he sound so reasonable? He'd only had a couple of hours sleep more than she had. "Just cut down a bit, that's all."

Laura sighed and looked at her watch. "How long is this going to take?" she asked.

"Hopefully, not too long," Nate said. "We just have to be patient. You know that."

"Maybe we should head back," Laura said. "Someone will come get us when he's ready. In the meantime, we can call the families, at least, get them to tell us about any other near death experiences."

"I agree, but…"

"Alright!"

This announcement was coupled with the dramatic throwing open of the door to the interview room. Nate, Laura, and the officer who was standing outside the door to prevent their suspect escaping all jumped.

The lawyer was standing there with a wide, arrogant grin. "You can come in and do your interview, now, agents."

"How kind of you," Laura said sarcastically. "We'll call the families after, Nate. Let's go."

Nate nodded and followed her, stifling a smile at her reaction to the lawyer. They entered the interview room and saw him: Pace Christinsin sitting there smugly behind the table, all but smirking at them as they took their seats.

Laura had a bad vibe from him, like she had from the start. There was a feeling in the pit of her stomach that was getting even worse, like something here was terribly wrong. What had he cooked up with this lawyer...?

"Alright," the lawyer said, sitting down next to his client and folding his hands together in front of him. "I believe you wish to know my client's whereabouts last night, on Friday night, and on Wednesday night – the dates corresponding to the murders in town."

Who was asking the questions in this interview. "That's right," Nate said, much to Laura's annoyance. This lawyer was so slimy, she didn't want to give him a single inch. She had a feeling he was the type to take a mile.

The lawyer made a hand gesture as if to clear the way for Christinsin to respond.

"I've just returned home from a trip out of state," Christinsin announced smugly. "I got back late last night – after the murder was reported."

Laura stared at him for a long moment.

"I'm sorry," she said. "I think I may have just had a temporary stroke, because I'm sure I heard you say you were giving us an alibi for the times of the murders."

"That's right," Christinsin crowed. "It's all recorded on security footage, credit card usage, everything you can possibly think of. I've been staying at a hotel. There's no way I could possibly have got back here in time to be involved with any one of the murders."

Under the table, Laura clenched her fists. "Then why didn't you say that at your home, instead of insisting on coming here and calling a lawyer?" she asked.

"See how it feels to have your time wasted?" Christinsin jeered. "Now you know how I felt when I got dragged in here for asking questions. Just asking questions! You'd think we live in a fascist state!"

"What is your problem?" Nate snapped. "We were having a calm conversation at your home – we didn't need to do all of this."

"I guess I just have a thing about cops," he sneered.

"Well, I'm sure you can spend a lot of time contemplating that feeling of having your time wasted," Laura said furiously, standing up so abruptly that her chair scraped across the floor. "On top of the assault on an FBI agent charge, we also have to check your alibi in great detail. Every last single person that could have seen you, every camera that might have captured you – we'll have to go through them all. That should be worth a night in the cells here at least, and possibly a very nice big fine. Don't you think?" This last was addressed to the lawyer, who turned a slightly contrite shade of pale, waving a hand quickly to stop his client from responding in any manner.

Laura stormed out of the interview room with Nate hot on her heels, then strode right down the hall without pausing. She was so angry she couldn't stop. She went to the stairs and walked up instead of waiting for the elevator, her anger taking her the way up to the roof even though it was a few more floors than she would normally have liked to walk – particularly on a night of no sleep.

It was when she got to the top that she let out a frustrated scream, directing it at the pigeons nesting there who scattered into the air in fright.

"Woah!" Nate said from behind her, quickly shoving a loose brick into the doorframe so that it wouldn't close and lock them out.

"Sorry," Laura muttered, rubbing her forehead as she paced back and forth restlessly. "Just – how could he do that? People are dying and he just, what, wanted to play a prank on us?"

"It's not your fault, Laura," Nate said.

Laura stared at him. "What's not my fault?"

"The fact that Haydn Townsend died." Nate moved over to the edge of the roof, leaning on the railing that separated them from the ground far, far below. "It's not your fault. We weren't here long enough to get to grips with the case yet."

"I don't have to get to grips with the case," Laura argued. "I just have to see the right clue. I…"

She stopped, feeling a vibration against her side. She dug in her pocket and drew out her cell phone, then cursed when she saw the name on the screen.

"What is it?" Nate asked.

Laura put the phone to her ear and pasted a faux cheery note into her voice. "Chief Rondelle!" she greeted him, and a cloud passed over Nate's face at the realization as well.

"Agent Frost," their boss replied. "I've just come into my office and saw the word about the new victim that cropped up last night."

"That's right, sir," Laura replied. She was about to add more, but she didn't even get the chance.

"Didn't I tell you that time was of the essence and you needed to act before he struck again? Damnit!" Rondelle exploded down the other end of the line. "I haven't even seen a press conference from you! Have you even warned local residents of the specific dangers? Agent Frost, this is unacceptable!"

Laura winced. Nate's eyebrows rose, and she shook her head. This was bad.

"Sir, we're doing everything we can right now," Laura said. "We've been up all night and just brought in our latest suspect for interview a short while ago."

"And?"

"Um…" Laura trailed off, not knowing what he expected her to say next.

"And, is he your killer?"

"Well," Laura said, her eyes going to the sky. She wished she could come up with a really great excuse, but she didn't have time to think. "No, sir, but that's another avenue of investigation cleared."

"If you're going to rule out every single person in the world that it's not before you catch him, then you're going to wind up with half the population of the city dead," Rondelle thundered. "When they called us for help, I assured them I was putting my best and fastest agents on the case. Are you making me a liar over there?"

"No, sir," Laura said, glancing at Nate and shaking her head slightly, shocked this time at how far Rondelle was going. Over the last few months he'd been running hot and cold, more often than not prone to snapping and shouting, in no mood for any kind of joking around. Now he actually sounded really angry.

"Then get on with it!" Rondelle concluded, and the line went dead.

"I guess he's not happy," Nate said.

"No," Laura replied. She briefly considered throwing her cell phone off the edge of the roof and watching it smash under the wheels of cars far below. "No, he isn't. And we need to come up with another angle on all of this – fast."

103

CHAPTER EIGHTEEN

Chris Fallow scrubbed his hands in the sink, making sure to thoroughly clean all parts of his fingers, palms, and even his lower arms and wrists before switching off the tap with an elbow. It was a practiced move, and one that he had undertaken so many times in his career as a surgeon.

Which was good, because he needed every ounce of power his brain had right now to focus on something else: the dilemma of what to do about Laura's note.

He replayed it in his mind, repeating the words that he had already memorized since he first read them. *Don't give George Elwood – your emergency patient – atropine today. He's allergic, but you'll only find out when the records come in after already administering it. L x*

He hadn't needed to ask around to figure out who had left the note. Only Laura would say something so cryptic and leave it attached to his door. Only Laura would, logically, try to tell him about something that was supposed to happen in the future.

He'd been wracking his brains over it all day long. First of all, he didn't have anyone scheduled in by the name of George Elwood, but since Laura had called him an emergency patient, that had made sense. He had told himself again and again that it was nothing, that she was just trying to mess with his head – or maybe back up her delusions. When this Elwood never materialized, she would give him some line like her warning in itself had been enough to deter the future she had seen from happening.

Only, then a mystery patient in need of emergency heart surgery had come in, and Chris had realized he needed to scrub in and start giving treatment, and he didn't know what to do about it. So, he had an emergency patient. That still didn't mean it was the one that Laura had told him about. But without a name attached to the man, he had no way of knowing.

Which was the genius of it, really, if Laura really was trying to mess with his mind.

But now he had a decision to make, because even doing nothing was still choosing to do something. He had information which might save a patient's life. Wherever it came from, if it was accurate, he had a duty to use it. It was just that he had no idea whether it really was accurate.

He could just say nothing and let life take its course.

But if the patient died on the table because of an allergic reaction that Chris had the power to prevent...

Could he really forgive himself for that?

He walked into the surgical suite to a flurry of activity that was already taking place around the prone body of the emergency patient who had been brought in.

"Pushing atropine," one of the other members of the team said, holding up a syringe, ready to inject it right away.

"No!" Chris said, so loud and so abrupt that everyone stopped and stared at him. "No, not atropine. We should go for an alternative."

The other man blinked at him. "Are you sure? Why?"

"I just..." Chris looked down at the patient. He was glad the surgical mask covered most of his face, hid his facial expression. He wished he had a good excuse. What was he supposed to say to explain this? "Please, I have a feeling. Just humor me on this. It won't harm him to use a different drug."

His colleague shrugged and turned back to a tray of prepared medicines. "Have it your way, he said, dropping the syringe of atropine into a hazard disposal bin.

Chris felt a momentary wave of relief at the thought that the atropine was gone. Somehow, even without proof, he knew. He just knew.

Laura was right.

Even so, there was fear – because if Laura wasn't right, if his own judgement in this case was wrong, then he was about to administer medicine to a patient without justification. And if the patient still died... there would be questions.

And there was fear, too, that Laura *was* right.

Because what did that mean, if she really could do the things she said she could do?

He blinked his eyes to try to clear his mind, reaching for a scalpel from the tray beside him. There was something more important to focus on right now. All other considerations floated away as he prepared to do his job – the thing he was best at.

He could think about the implications later.

"Are you sure this is the right file?" Chris asked, holding it up to show the nurse. She glanced over and then nodded.

"Yep, that's definitely it."

Chris pondered it for another moment, pursing his lips, folding his arms, and then unfolding them. "It's just – this says his name is George Elwood, and he's allergic to atropine."

"That's right," the nurse replied, sounding a touch bored. "Just like you said."

"Right." Chris shook his head, rubbed a hand over his forehead.

"What's wrong?" the nurse asked. "You made the right call. If he'd been given the atropine, he would have died. You must be pleased that he's in recovery, surely?"

"Of course, I am," Chris said, his voice then dropping to a mutter. "I just don't know how."

"You said you had a feeling, right? You didn't actually know he was allergic?" the nurse asked.

"Yeah." Chris felt bad for not telling the whole truth, but half the truth was already wild enough. "I just feel a bit weirded out, I guess."

"That's just doctor's intuition," she confided. "I've known a good few cases where it saved a life. I've even had it come up a couple of times, myself."

"Right," Chris nodded, as if this was actually any kind of explanation. "Right, that must be it. Anyway, I'm heading out."

The nurse smiled as she took the file back, and Chris turned away. He was already wearing his coat and carrying his briefcase, so she had no reason to question him as he walked in the direction that would eventually take him towards the exit.

She had no way to know the turmoil that was going on inside his head. No way to understand how conflicted he was.

Because he had done the right thing. He'd trusted Laura's word, and she had been right, and together through that they had saved a life.

But it was the implications that were weighing heavy on him now. Because if Laura was right about the information – right down to the patient's name and the day he would come in for an unplanned emergency procedure, as well as the precise drug that he was allergic to – then she had to have known it somehow. And there was no way anyone could have known that, no matter how good an investigator they were. It was a thing that hadn't happened yet, and before it happened, there had been no indication that it would.

So, what he had to answer now – a doctor, a man of science, of facts – was how someone could possibly have known what would happen in the future before it did. Not in vague terms, like how a fortune teller would use cold reading to supply something that sounded right for everyone. But in real terms. In facts. In things that couldn't be confused or fudged.

Right now, the only thing that Chris could possibly think of as an explanation was that she had been telling the truth about all of it.

Everything.

Including the fact that she had psychic powers.

And he wasn't sure yet if he could reconcile that reality with the one he could see, hear, taste, and touch around him – and if he couldn't accept something that had literally been proven to him, then he wasn't sure how he could live in his current reality at all.

CHAPTER NINETEEN

Laura groaned, giving up and just putting both of her hands flat on top of the desk, covering as many of the photographs as possible. "It's not working," she said.

"Are you sure you were just touching the photo before?" Nate asked. "There wasn't any other particular trigger, anything else you had to do to make it work?"

"I would be the one to know," Laura said, glaring at him and then regretting it. "Sorry. I didn't do anything particular. I just touched the photo."

"Okay, well, maybe there aren't any more visions to be had from the photos, then," Nate said, not unreasonably. "We need to try something else."

"But what?" Laura asked. She rubbed her eyes, frustrated, and tired and sick at heart. Chris wasn't talking to her, Rondelle was on the warpath, someone else had died before they stopped the killer, and now she couldn't figure out how to trigger a vision or where to go from here. And they were waiting for the two families to come in, having figured it would be quicker to get Cortez to arrange it all while they carried on working, a decision that now struck Laura as wasteful on time.

"The family members," Nate said. "Maybe they'll bring something you can touch. Medical records or something. I don't know."

"Who brings a copy of their murdered loved one's medical records to a police interview without being asked to?" Laura asked, staring at him.

Nate shrugged. "Okay, fine. I'm just trying to come up with ideas."

Laura closed her eyes for a moment, trying to breathe. Trying to remember who she was actually mad at: the killer. Not Nate. Not her boss, who had targets and pressure as well. Not even herself, even if it felt that way pretty often.

There was a knock at the door.

"Yes?" Nate shouted.

Sergeant Cortez put her head inside the family interview room. "I just thought you'd want to know. Genevieve Granger is here."

"Send her in," Larua said, hastily sweeping all the photographs from the crime scene into a pile and then shutting the folder to hide them away.

Not a moment too soon, as the grieving widow then entered and crossed the room to sit on the comfortable sofa opposite them; had they been left out, she would have easily been able to see the photographic evidence of her wife's dead body.

"Thank you for coming in," Laura said right away, trying to switch herself into that more compassionate mode so there was no risk of her snapping at Ginny. "We wanted to give you some updates and talk a little more about Jessika and her work."

"Of course." Ginny dropped onto the seat and placed her purse beside her, then looked at them expectantly. Her face was still pale, marked by the tracks of grief. She looked thin and small. Like the last few days had already diminished her so much.

"I'm afraid the first update we have is not positive news," Nate said, his tone suitably grave. "We have identified a further victim of the same killer, who was murdered last night in a very similar manner to Jessika and Brooke Ware."

Ginny gasped, her hand going to cover her mouth. "When are you going to stop him?" she burst out, her words slightly muffled.

"We're doing everything we can, and we've already questioned and released several suspects," Nate said. Laura was glad he'd taken the question because she wasn't sure how sincerely she could answer it herself. "I know it's difficult to hear, but we have a lot of hands on deck here and we're following every single line of inquiry very seriously."

Ginny seemed to accept this, nodding wanly. "You said you had more questions for me?"

"Yes," Laura said. "It's about Jessika's work. I understand that she worked with primarily patients who had gone through a near death experience. What was the inspiration behind that? Had she been through one herself?"

Ginny's eyes opened wider in surprise. "Yes," she said. "Yes, she did. Is that relevant?"

"Well, it may be," Laura said, not wanting to give too much away, excitement thrumming under her skin. "It's a line of inquiry we're following. Can you tell me about that event?"

"It was about ten years ago," Ginny said. "She was trying to get home during a storm and she was hit by lightning. Her heart actually stopped, but just by total coincidence, there was an off-duty EMT driving by who saw her fall to the ground. He called backup while he saved her life and got her heart going again, and they got her to hospital quickly enough that she recovered fully."

Laura's own heart was racing now. They'd been right. The near death experience was the link. This was what connected everything. Now they just needed to know how that factor connected to the killer, and they would have him.

"Oh!" Ginny exclaimed, cutting through Laura's winding-up of the interview. She suddenly dove into her purse and pulled out a small wallet. She rifled through it for a moment and then took out a small silver coin, holding it out. Laura took it without knowing what it was, a pulse of pain striking through her head like thunder as she did so.

"Jessika gave me -"

Laura was looking into her face. Jessika. But she was alive now, not pale and dead as she had been on the coroner's slab.

She was alive and vibrant, moving out to the sidewalk as she locked up her building's door behind her. She turned to walk towards her car, getting out her keys. It was clear that she was only thinking about getting home, seeing her wife, eating dinner, having some rest.

Until the wire twisted around her neck and she was yanked back, out of Laura's line of sight, gone. And Laura knew to what end.

And like a blink, without any warning, she was there again. Jessika Granger walking down the street, much younger, carefree, a purse on her shoulder and her long hair swaying behind her. There was a storm rolling overhead, heavy clouds rumbling, rain lashing down, but Jessika had an umbrella over her head and didn't seem to mind. She even smiled, tilting her head back just enough to avoid getting wet and looking up at the sky. A car went by and splashed through the puddles near the gutter and she shrieked as she dodged the water. Then she laughed, mostly to herself, shaking her head and walking on down the street as if the storm didn't bother her at all.

There was a flash of lightning, close by – too close. Jessika's face pinched, her steps faltered. A moment later there was a crash of thunder, so loud she winced.

And then the rain stopped.

Jessika frowned in confusion, hearing the sound of the rain hitting her umbrella stop. She moved it to the side, looking up at the sky, her face lighting up in wonder at the fact that everything was suddenly dry.

And then an arc of cold light flew down from the sky and hit her, and she screamed and flew into the air, and Laura inhaled the pungent smell of burnt flesh –

"This," Ginny said. "She was carrying it in her purse when the lightning struck her. She said it was lucky because she hadn't died. I always laughed and said maybe it was unlucky because she got hit by lightning in the first place, but she insisted I carry it with me after we first moved in together."

"Then you should keep it safe now," Laura said, her voice tight with strange emotion. She handed it back firmly, pressing it into Ginny's palm so there was no risk of dropping it. "Was there anything else related to near death experiences that Jessika was involved in? I know that she worked with other survivors, but was there something else? For example, a support group, or an online forum, or something like that?"

Ginny thought for a long moment. "Yes," she said at last. "Yes, there was something. There was a book."

"A book?" Laura repeated.

"This was, um…" Ginny screwed up her nose and shook her head. "I don't know. Two years ago? Three? Anyway, someone approached her for comment in a book about near death experiences, and she ended up doing a whole interview with them. She was used as one of the case studies. It was pretty cool, actually."

"What was the name of the book?" Laura asked immediately. "And the author, if you remember?"

"Oh, yeah, it was something like… I don't know, something like *The Secrets of Near Death* or *Near Death Secrets* or something like that. And the author was a local man – this Sean Jardine. I remember him pretty well. He came by the house a number of times for the interviews, and we went to the book launch party too."

Laura glanced at Nate and saw him jotting down the name and title in his notebook, meaning that she didn't have to. "That's great," she said. "We're going to look into this connection, so thank you for providing all of that information."

"That's all we need for now," Nate said. "If you find any more information at home, or a copy of the book, please do let us know – it would be great to read it."

"I'll go see if I can find it," Ginny nodded. "Jess had a lot of books, so it might take me a while to look through them all, but I'll hand it in as soon as I can grab it."

"Thank you," Nate nodded. He got up, shadowing Ginny to the door, his hand hovering in the air behind her to guide her along. "I hope that next time we speak, we'll be able to provide you a more concrete update."

Ginny nodded. She looked for a moment like she was going to say something, but then she closed her mouth and nodded and disappeared into the hall.

Nate closed the door after her and looked back at Laura, who was still sitting on the sofa.

"You saw something?" he asked.

Laura looked up at him with a wan smile, feeling the headache pulse inside her temple as she moved her head. She was tired enough already – the visions coming on top of one another weren't helping. "I did."

"You need something for the pain?" Nate asked perceptively.

"Maybe." Laura cleared her throat. "I brought some, at the desk…"

"Wait here."

Nate was gone before Laura could even react or tell him to wait. She hated feeling helpless, like she needed to be looked after. On the other hand, there was undeniably something nice – like a guilty pleasure – about being waited on hand and foot, having someone fuss over you. She rested, propping her head in her hands, before the door opened again and Nate pushed a glass of water and a pill in front of her face.

Laura took them gratefully, swallowing the pill with a mouthful of water and then nodding her thanks. Nate set the glass down and sat beside her. "So?"

"It was two deaths again, just like with Townsend," Laura said. The intervening moments and the time to analyze what she had seen were useful in being able to explain it. "I saw her being strangled – attacked, just like we knew. It was kind of a different angle from the security footage, but all the same. And then I saw her walk down the street and get struck by lightening exactly as Ginny described it."

"We just need to hear what happened to Brooke and we'll be there," Nate said. "If this is a definite trend, one of the first things we need to figure out is how the killer is identifying the victims. You think the book could be a link somehow? Or that Jessika might have been part of some kind of group that Ginny didn't know about?"

"I would be very interested in going through their social media accounts," Laura nodded. "Maybe something like a Facebook group where survivors share stories and coping strategies. I imagine that if Jessika was part of one of those, it would be a really great way to get referrals for patients."

"You're right about that," Nate nodded. "I saw Cortez out there – she has Bree Ware with her."

"Okay," Laura nodded. "Let's do it."

"Are you sure?" Nate asked. "Your painkillers can't possibly have kicked in yet."

Laura smiled at him, trying to make it a braver one than last time. "I'll be fine. I've been doing this for a while, you know."

Nate made a grunting noise low in his throat which sounded like a disagreement, but he got up and went to the door anyway. He made a motioning movement while leaning out into the hall, and before long, Cortez appeared there with Bree Ware beside her.

"Hi," Bree said, and there was none of the fire she'd had yesterday. Today she looked defeated and tired and ill. She was clearly progressing through the different phases of this process. Laura was relieved – Bree had been so confrontational before that she hadn't been looking forward to the interview.

"Miss Ware," Laura said. "Please, take a seat."

Bree moved over and sat, moving her purse in front of her. She was wearing a long knitted cardigan, with sleeves that covered her hands.

"We just wanted to speak with you about some leads we've discovered," Nate said. "The questions might seem random, but every little bit of information we can get is really going to help."

"Okay," Bree said. She seemed hesitant, restrained. Laura thought she probably felt a little embarrassed at how she had snapped at them yesterday, only to realize that it was her sister's own fault that her records didn't show what she'd thought they had.

"Did your sister ever have a near death experience?" Nate asked. "Before this, I mean."

Bree frowned. "No, she never had anything like that. I don't think she ever even broke a bone."

Laura froze, her heart stopping in her chest for a second.

No?

If the answer was no, then…

Laura's head span. She had been so sure that they had finally figured out the connection. If Brooke Ware didn't fit the pattern, then quite simply, the pattern they thought they were building was wrong.

How could her visions match up perfectly to everything, and yet the theory was wrong?

She hadn't had a vision for Brooke yet. Hadn't seen a single death, let alone two. Unless Bree had brought something that belonged to her sister without being asked, there was little chance of it happening right now, either – and Laura needed answers to make sense of this.

"Are you absolutely sure?" Nate asked with a frown. He shifted slightly, and Laura knew he felt the same tension about this. Only not quite the same – because she was the one who had seen the visions and come up with the theory, and if she was wrong, this was all her fault for sending them on a wild goose chase.

"Yes, I'm sure," Bree said, making Laura's heart sink even further. "She even – oh, God. Is that what this is all about?"

"What?" Laura asked, sitting up straight.

"The book?" Bree asked, looking between Nate and Laura.

The two agents looked at each other, too.

"What book?" Nate asked, though Laura knew he must be feeling the same racing hope that she had, the same heartbeat turned up to eleven at the thought that maybe their theory was back on.

Bree groaned and covered her eyes. "It's so embarrassing," she said. "A few years ago, Brooke did this – I don't know, like a prank I guess. She was interviewed for this book about people who had nearly died and lived to talk about it. It never happened to her, though. She just made it all up. She had a real laugh about it."

Laura blinked. A fake near death experience?

But that would mean...

"This book," Laura said. "Was it written by a man called Sean Jardine?"

"Yes, that's right!" Bree replied. "How did you know that? Is it all linked to the book somehow? Did something happen with it?"

"We don't know just yet," Laura said, not wanting to get ahead of herself. "What I can tell you is that the suspect you spoke to us about yesterday has been cleared, so we are looking at different avenues now." That was vague enough, she felt, but at least would stop the remaining Wares from going after the stalker themselves and doing something stupid.

"Well, who do you think did it now?" Bree asked. Her eyes widened. "Not... Sean Jardine?"

Laura managed to stop a growl of frustration from ripping out of her throat. She was already worried about the reaction the Wares would

114

have to the first suspect given their anger yesterday. Giving them another one to focus on instead had not been her intention.

"We don't have a specific suspect we can talk about at this time," Laura said. "We've only just heard about the book, so it's too early to say whether it's relevant to the case or not." Again, her word choice was careful: she didn't want to admit to Bree that she wasn't the first person to mention the book, or that it was connected to the other victims as well.

"Thank you for coming in," Nate said hastily. "I don't suppose you've thought of anything new to add since our conversation before?"

"I haven't," Bree said, shaking her head and deflating again. "It still just doesn't make any sense."

"Try not to hang all your hopes on it making sense," Nate said, though his voice was soft. "When we're dealing with killers, often, their motives and reasoning are pretty different from what we would think of as normal. If it makes you feel better, you can focus on getting justice – but if it was me losing a loved one, I'd try to think more about the good times we did have together than the reason or the story for why they were killed."

Bree looked at him hard. "But you haven't ever lost a loved one, have you?" she asked, her tone flat.

Nate swallowed hard.

"Thank you, Miss Ware," Laura said, this time jumping in to save Nate. She stood up and her head did not feel like a steel ball was ricocheting around inside of it, which she took to mean the painkillers were working. "We'll be in touch as soon as we have any new updates to pass on."

"Right," Bree said, standing up to join her. She went towards the door without much resistance, though Laura could feel something running through her – like a current. Anger. It was still there, right under the surface. Maybe it just wasn't aimed at law enforcement anymore.

Laura closed the door behind her, and made a mental note to ask Cortez to have their assigned family detective watch them extremely closely.

"This is it," Nate said, now they were alone again. He had pulled his cell phone out of his pocket and was tapping the screen. "Isn't it? The book. It has to be the link. Jessika Granger and Brooke Ware were both interviewed for it – it's the only link between them. So, if our killer is going after people who had near death experiences, then he must be using a copy of this book to identify them."

"We need to get our hands on a copy and find out if Haydn Townsend is in it," Laura said. "The way I see it, if he isn't, then he has to be the victim with the personal connection to the killer. And if he is included inside the book, then we know that everyone else featured is under threat."

Nate was scrolling through something on his cell phone. He frowned, biting his lip for a moment. "I can't find anything online by Sean Jardine," he said, then his face lit up. "Oh! I have it… wait, hang on. It says there's none in stock."

"It's out of print after only a few years," Laura said. "It must not have been very popular. Which narrows the field of potential killers, but on the other hand, might make it harder for us to find a copy."

"Well, there's one way I can think of to get a copy of that book as fast as possible," Nate said, looking up at her. He grinned. "Let's go meet Sean Jardine."

Laura opened her hand to show him the car keys. "Way ahead of you," she said, opening the interview room door again to lead the way out.

CHAPTER TWENTY

Laura parked the car and looked up. The sun was fully up now, people already moving around and leaving their homes to go to work. They were going to have to cross their fingers that Sean Jardine was home, because they had no information about his potential current employers – only an address.

"Are you sure this is it?" Laura asked. The property was almost on the verge of being dilapidated. It might have been a nice home once, but now it was in dire need of repairs: paint peeling on the door, weeds growing in the front yard, a broken window patched up with cardboard. It was dirty, covered in a gray sheen as if someone had sprayed the whole place with something disgusting. There was even mail spilling out of the mailbox, which was crumpled and half-broken off its perch.

"This is the address we were given," Nate said, double-checking the GPS and the details he had written down. "Doesn't exactly look like the home of a successful writer."

"Then maybe he wasn't successful," Laura guessed, taking a breath, and then getting out of the car to find out.

The two of them walked in what suddenly felt like strange silence to the door. The whole neighborhood was quiet, like it was holding its breath. Laura felt like she was being watched, glancing up quickly to try to justify the sensation. She was sure she saw a curtain twitch in one of the upstairs windows, as though someone had jerked away quickly.

There was a faded, dirty sign on the door, printed on plain paper, telling callers not to bother the homeowner unless they had been invited. Laura ignored it and knocked loudly, defying Jardine not to come to the door. He didn't have to. They could come inside to him, if they really needed to.

"This is creepy," Nate muttered as quietly as he could.

Laura resisted the urge to smirk at him – largely because she was finding it a little creepy, too.

There was a long pause and then the door opened – by a crack. Just the tiniest amount, enough for them to see…

Nothing. The house was so dark inside, despite the bright morning, that Laura couldn't even make out more than the vague shape of a person behind the door.

"Sean Jardine?" she guessed, anyway.

"What do you want?" he asked, his voice a dark mutter. Laura wasn't even convinced she had heard it after the sound faded away.

"We need to talk to you about your book," she said.

There was a long pause. The door opened a tiny fraction more. "Are you publishers?" he asked.

"No," Laura said. "We're agents."

The door opened fully, revealing Sean Jardine for the first time. He was tall and of a medium to strong build, as though he looked after his own body far better than he did the house – though his clothing was stained and even ripped in a couple of places. There were dark shadows smudged under his eyes and his dark hair was unruly, as though he hadn't combed or neatened it in a while.

"Okay," he said, stepping aside.

Nate moved forward, lifting up his badge as he did so. "FBI agents," he clarified.

Jardine swore and tried to slam the door shut, but Nate's foot – in a black, heavy boot that could handle the stress – was already in the way. With a wide and determined grin, Nate pushed the door back open all the way.

"I think it's best we come inside for a chat," he said, and there was enough menace in his voice that Jardine actually stepped back and led the way.

He took them into a room that, like the outside of the house, had seen better days. The once-cream carpet was dotted with all manner of stains in a range of different colors, from what looked like red wine to black patches to even a singed area. At least, Laura hoped the deep red was wine.

There were empty beer cans crushed all over the coffee table and under it, as well as empty takeout containers, and a blanket on the sofa hinted that Jardine had taken to passing out down there. Laura eyed the empty cans and then made herself look away. Now was not the time to be getting tempted.

"I don't need to speak to you," Jardine declared, crossing his arms over his chest. He didn't sit, instead remaining standing and facing Nate, as if expecting a confrontation. Laura glanced at the stained and dirty sofa and chair and decided that standing was probably the right decision all round. "You can't make me speak to you. I'm not giving away anything. I know about these cases, where someone comes and gets all the ideas and then produces it quicker. I'm not giving you my IP."

"Your IP?" Laura said blankly.

"Don't play dumb," Jardine snapped. "You're here to steal my new book idea."

"We really are FBI agents, not book agents," Laura said, taking her own badge out this time to show him. She stepped closer so he could examine it, then further away to give him his space once he seemed to be done.

"I still don't need to speak to you," Jardine said. One of his eyes seemed to twitch.

"You don't have to," Laura said. "But we'd like to rule you out as a suspect in a murder inquiry, so I would really advise that you do."

Like everything else, it was a test. If he was innocent, he would likely talk with them, realizing that the accusation was a serious one. If he was guilty, then he would know that talking with him wouldn't rule him out. He would either get extremely nervous and try to lie – or he would still refuse to talk to them outright.

"It's a free country," Jardine snapped. "I can do what I like."

Laura sighed. This was going to go like that, was it? At least this was all increasing the likelihood that he was the man they wanted, after all. And if he was the killer, then she would take any amount of hassle to take him off the streets.

"You interviewed some local people for your book about near death experiences," Laura said. "Do you remember their names?"

Jardine wrinkled up his face. "I spoke to them personally and spent long hours transcribing their interviews, and then I spent time publicizing the book... of course I remember what their names are."

"Okay," Laura said. "So?"

Jardine stared at her.

"Let's see," Laura continued. "Do you remember talking to a Jessika Granger?"

"Yes," he said. "Yeah, the lightning girl. Why?"

"Do you watch the news, Mr. Jardine?" Nate asked, gesturing with a thumb back towards the TV in the corner.

"It doesn't work," Jardine muttered. "What? What's going on?"

"You really don't know what might have happened to Jessika to put her in the news this week?" Laura asked. She was finding it a little hard

119

to believe. By this point, everyone they'd spoken to had heard about Brooke Ware, and now that time had passed, they were aware of Granger as well.

Jardine sighed in annoyance. "Just tell me so you can get the hell out of my home," he said.

Laura raised her eyebrows at the way he'd spoken to them, but she complied. "She's dead, Mr. Jardine."

There was a pause in which he seemed to consider it. Then he shrugged. "Okay," he said. "So?"

"That doesn't distress you at all?" Nate asked. "Or even surprise you?"

"Of course, it's sad," he said. "I didn't really know her. She's not the first person I interviewed to die, either."

"No?" Laura asked. He was talking too much, incriminating himself. That was good. She wasn't going to interrupt him if he was working his way towards a confession.

"Some of them were older," he said. He scratched the back of his neck like it was nothing. Casual. "There was one guy who just died of old age. And Brooke."

Laura stared at him. He hadn't heard about Jessika, but he knew about Brooke?

"Brooke?" Nate prompted, taking the thought right out of Laura's head.

"Brooke Ware," he elaborated, confirming her suspicions entirely.

"I thought you said your TV wasn't working and you hadn't seen the news lately," Laura said.

Jardine looked at her blankly. "Did I?"

Laura exchanged a look with Nate. He nodded. This conversation was getting dangerous already. If he said something really important and he hadn't already been read his rights, the lawyers would have a field day in court. And by the way Jardine was talking, lying, and then proving himself a liar one sentence later, it would be essential to have a tape recording to play in court if he didn't confess. Something that showed how he was already tying himself into knots trying to hide the truth. They needed to do this right.

"Sean Jardine," Laura said. "I'm placing you under arrest for murder." She stepped forward with handcuffs and began to recite his rights, but she barely got another word out before Sean moved quick as a flash out of her way, leaping over the back of the sofa.

"No! I didn't do anything!" he yelled, but Nate quickly stepped out into the hall – between Jardine and the front door. There was a moment in which Laura clearly saw Jardine hesitate, searching for an answer. Then he dashed forward again, moving in a strange way from a complete stop to complete motion – towards the stairs.

Laura admitted that, given the lack of a back door in the house, it was the only option – but it didn't seem a particularly smart one.

He was already close by, so Nate was the first one to start leaping up the stairs after him. Laura wasn't far behind, the two of them both charging after Jardine's mad run. The carpet was worn threadbare in some places on the stairs and Laura nearly tripped on a loose flap of the fabric, but she recovered and kept close on Nate's heels. From their position they could easily see Jardine rush to one side, enter a room, and slam the door shut – and then they heard the click of a lock sliding into place.

"Great." Laura threw her hands up in the air. "Is that the bathroom?"

Nate glanced around, checking out the other rooms. "I think so."

"Then he probably has razors in there," she said, mouthing the word 'razors' instead of saying it out loud just in case she would have given Jardine an idea. "We need to get inside fast."

"Okay, probable cause," Nate said, shrugging. "Move away from the door."

Laura did as she was told, stepping to the side. "Jardine!" she shouted, making sure he wouldn't be able to say he couldn't hear their warnings. "Get away from the door, now!"

Nate squared his shoulders, sized up the door, and then leaned back to give himself some momentum. With a grunt of effort, he kicked his leg at full power directly into the part of the door right below the handle, where the lock was located.

The second kick did the trick. The wood splintered and burst inwards, collapsing under the force Nate threw into it, and the door swung open. On the other side, Jardine was there, turning towards them with a look of surprise and shock – and most of all, frustration that he hadn't managed to get away. He had been in the process, apparently, of trying to force a tiny, half-blocked bathroom window open wide enough to fit his body through it. Only his leg had made it through so far, and even that looked like a tight fit.

"Get down," Laura said, done with the nonsense he was trying to pull off.

"You can't take me in," Jardine said, his eyes wide, as he scrabbled at the window again. There was paint over the edges, and it didn't budge an inch.

"Yeah, I think we can," Laura said, handing her cuffs to Nate as he walked forward to grab their suspect and literally pull him back from the edge.

The fight seemed to go out of him as soon as the cuffs were on. Laura turned away to lead the way downstairs – but as she did, a bedroom caught her eye. Why not check it out, she thought, while they were here anyway, to see if there was any evidence?

One thing stood out as soon as she stepped inside, one ear on the slow progress of Nate and Jardine down the stairs as Nate repeatedly had to order him to take each individual step.

The book. It was sitting on a small display stand near his bed, one of the only things in the whole house that wasn't grimy or broken or neglected in some other way. Laura walked over and picked it up, tapping it against her other hand thoughtfully. They had a copy now.

Time to find out just what about this book was so groundbreaking that someone had ended up dead.

***

Laura folded her arms and leaned back in the chair, looking across the table at Jardine. Beside her, Nate was equally quiet and serious.

"So," Laura said. "Tell me about the book."

Jardine scoffed. "Waste of time!" he said.

"We'll be the judge of whether it's worth talking about," Laura said.

"No," Jardine replied. "I mean, writing the book was a waste of time. I never earned out my advance, and I'd already spent all of that on the interviews and research and all the time it took. Sent myself in circles getting it edited and polished. And after all that, it goes out of print before I even earn another cent."

"It's out of print?" Laura raised an eyebrow. "That must have been very frustrating."

"Yes," Jardine declared. "I wanted to throw it out of a window."

"You didn't, though," Laura pointed out. She tapped the cover of the book they had taken from beside his bed. "You kept it in prime position. Almost like a shrine to it."

"It's my work," he said, almost pompously, trying to fold his own arms and being stopped by a jingle of his cuffs. "Of course, I couldn't throw it away."

Laura held back the urge to point out that he'd been the one to bring up throwing it in the first place. She had the feeling that if she insisted on arguing logic with this particular suspect, she wasn't going to get anywhere.

"The interviews," Nate prompted. "You conducted three in particular we want to talk about."

"Which three?" Jardine asked, raising his eyebrows.

"The three who died recently," Laura said, leaving him enough of a hint to hang himself with. She wanted to know if he was going to mention the last name. Brooke and Jessika had been all over the news, and besides they'd given him the information already. But there was one more victim whose name Laura had seen in the book as she skimmed through the contents page: Haydn Townsend. And if Jardine brought up Townsend, then the game was up, because right now it was only the killer, the cops, and the family who knew he was dead.

"Brooke Ware," Jardine said. "Jessika Granger. And Herbie Warrington."

Laura blinked. "Herbie Warrington?" Her mind started to run overdrive. Had they missed a victim?

"Terribly sad," Jardine shrugged. "Heart attack. It can come for any of us, you know."

Laura squinted at him. Was he trying to play with them? Or did he really not realize they weren't talking about this heart attack victim? The fact that he hadn't given the right name wasn't proof in either direction; if he was the killer, he would have more than enough reason to try to mislead them.

"What about the interviews?" Laura prompted, trying to keep things on track. "Let's start with Brooke Ware."

"Oh, she was terribly sad," Jardne said. It was like he'd picked up the phrase 'terribly sad' and now didn't want to put it down. "Such a hard experience for such a young girl. She was only a young teen when it happened. I really felt for her. And she's pretty, too, so that helped with a few sales – we put her photo in with the press release."

Laura blinked at him again. She felt like she was getting whiplash with this guy. It was like he was paying lip service to the way he was supposed to react – to compassion, sadness, grief – but then revealing what he really thought in the same breath. Didn't he have any kind of filter?

"She was murdered," Laura said, trying to bring the conversation to a place they could use. "And we believe she was murdered because of the interview she gave in your book."

Jardine looked at her with a puzzled expression. "Why would someone do that?"

"Well, one theory is that the killer is targeting people who had near death experiences," Laura said.

"That makes sense," Jardine nodded sagely, even though everyone sitting at that table must have been able to understand that it didn't. Not really. It was the kind of twisted logic that a killer would have.

"There's just one thing," Nate said, clearly ready to drop a revelation and see how Jardine reacted. "She never had a near death experience."

Jardine frowned, opened his mouth, then closed it again. Laura analyzed every twitch of his facial muscles, every micro-movement. Was that guilt? Nervousness that he had struck the wrong victim? Or just pure confusion?

"Yes, she did," he said, finally. "I wrote about it."

"No, she lied to you," Nate said. The blunt words were designed to strike home, to get a reaction out of him. Anger or distress or whatever it might be. "She made the whole thing up. She never had a near death experience at all."

There was a long pause in which Jardine continued to only frown.

"Do you think that's why the sales weren't very good?" he asked at last.

Laura looked at Nate. She had to. She didn't get where this guy was coming from. She opened his file, tapping something on the first page. "Mr. Jardine, your records show that you have been diagnosed with a number of complex mental conditions," she said. "Can I ask how you're coping with those?"

Jardine made a kind of shrugging gesture. "I just keep to myself," he said.

Laura cocked her head to the side. "What about your medication?"

"Couldn't afford it." Jardine's fingers twitched together as if he were pointing with two of them, and his demeanor changed to a more cheerful one as if a switch had been flicked. "Hey, could I get a cigarette?"

"You can have a smoking break if you answer our questions fully," Nate said. "Do you have them on you?"

"Cigarettes? Oh no, I don't smoke," Jardine said, shrugging and letting his fingers fall slack again. "I just thought it might be fun. It feels right, doesn't it?"

Laura looked at Nate again. What was he doing?

Was this an act, or...

Was he really off his meds, unstable, and completely unsure of the severity of the situation he found himself in?

Laura knew she was going to regret asking it – knew she was only shooting herself in the foot. But there was a certain duty of care. And even if this man was a killer, and even if it was hard to be compassionate towards him for that reason, there was still the fact that an unsafe interview would never stand up in court.

"Why didn't you want to exercise your right to a lawyer, Mr. Jardine?" she asked.

"I don't know any lawyers," he said. "But it's okay. I won't get you in trouble about the door. I guess I overreacted by locking it. So long as you pay to fix it, I don't need a lawyer."

Laura looked at Nate and took a deep breath.

"This interview is suspended until you have representation and a medical check," she said, getting up and taking her file with her. Nate followed. She paused on the threshold of the door and looked back at Jardine. "Just stay there. Someone will come to talk with you soon."

Outside, Nate leaned against the wall, sighing, as Laura closed the door.

"I had to," Laura said. "I don't think he has even a single clue about what's going on right now."

"You're right," Nate said. "I just wish he'd made some casual offhand comment about how he strangled them, or something. So we could wrap this up nicely."

"I know," Laura said. "But I don't know if he did it, anyway."

Nate looked at her sharply. "What? But he fits everything. He's the right height and build; he knew all three of the victims personally. He clearly has a problem with that book not turning out as successful as he thought it would. He's got all the right signs."

"And yet," Laura said, shaking her head. "I don't know. Maybe he's a good actor. But it felt to me like he was way too out of touch with reality to be able to pull something like this off so well."

"I mean… maybe," Nate said. "But if you're right, then what are we supposed to do now? The day's getting late. We don't know if the killer is intending to strike again tonight. Not to mention Rondelle wants us to finish this up as quick as possible."

"I have an idea of where to start," Laura said, holding up the copy of the book with a determined look.

CHAPTER TWENTY ONE

Laura sat down at her desk and slapped the book down on it, gesturing to Nate's computer. "Are you ready?"

"Give me a chance," he swore, hurriedly sitting down and waking up his monitor. He rapidly typed in his login credentials and then nodded. "Okay, give me the first one."

"I have a Callie Scrivener," Laura said. "It says here she was thirty-eight at the time of the interview."

Nate typed rapidly on his keyboard. "Yep. I've got her. Looks like she's still local according to the most recent information. Date of birth matches up with that age range."

Laura flipped ahead through Booke Ware's interview. "Next one is Gus Tanner."

Nate type again. "Age?"

"No idea," Laura said. She skim-read the first few lines of the chapter. "He was seventeen when his near death experience happened, so I guess any age from that up."

"Gustavus Tanner," Nate said. "Got him! What a name. Alright, looks like he's moved out of state."

"He's safe, then," Laura said. "Right? I mean, how far out of state?"

"Way out of state," Nate said. "Like, a flight away."

"Great, then the killer isn't going to go that far to get to him," Laura said. "At least, not until he's already gone after Callie – might as well get the ones you can reach locally first."

"Agreed," Nate said. "Right, next one?"

Laura flipped past Jessika and the old man Jardine had mentioned, scanning the text for any other names. She didn't want to miss a potential victim because she hadn't realized they were mentioned as an aside in one of the interviews as someone with the same experience. "I have Clara Brand, twenty-two at the time of the interview."

"Got her," Nate said. "She's still local as well."

Laura flipped through the rest of the pages. "I haven't got anyone else that we haven't already heard of," she said. "One of those two women has to be the next victim."

"Next victim?"

Laura looked up to see Princess Detective standing right behind them, holding an instant coffee cup. "We're just covering our bases," she said.

"But you've got the killer in custody," Princess said. "Right? Everyone else has gone out to the bar to celebrate."

"Nice of them to invite us," Nate muttered.

"We may not," Laura said. "He hasn't confessed, and we haven't found any physical evidence yet. It pays to be cautious. What we do have is pretty concrete evidence on who the next two potential victims are."

"Oh!" the Princess replied. "So, you can protect those two instead of trying to go after another potential suspect."

"Right," Laura nodded. "We'd better give them a call. It's getting late already. We can warn them to be safe and send some patrol cars to hang around outside and make sure no one goes after them."

"I'll take Callie," Nate said. "You call Clara."

Laura nodded, taking a piece of paper from him as soon as he'd finished scrawling the number from his screen. She was oddly aware of the detective watching her, like she was a case study in a class. She dialed the number and waited, hearing the tone ring and ring and ring...

"Hello?"

"Hi, is that Clara Brand?" Laura asked. "You did an interview for a book called *Secrets Revealed: Near Death Experiences* by Sean Jardine?"

"Um, yes, that's me," she said on the other end of the line, sounding puzzled. Her voice was youthful, as expected.

"My name is Special Agent Laura Frost with the FBI," she said. "I'm calling as we believe you may be in danger. I'm sorry to be dramatic, but there is a killer attacking your fellow interviewees, and you are one of just two candidates left that he could go after."

"What?" There was a long moment of pause. Laura let Clara get her head around it a little before continuing.

"You've probably heard the details of a couple of them on the news this week," Laura said. "Unfortunately, this is very serious. I'm sending a patrol car to you now to keep an eye on you – where are you at the moment?"

"Oh, I'm at home," Clara said. "Oh, gosh. There's... there's really no need. I'm staying inside tonight. I don't want to waste your resources."

"It's not a waste," Laura said. "We really think you could be in serious danger."

"Well, did the killer break into anyone else's house?" Clara asked.

"… No," Laura admitted.

"I'll keep the windows and doors locked and stay upstairs," Clara declared. "Even if someone comes to the door, I won't answer. What about tomorrow?"

"Unless you hear from us, I think it's a good idea for you to stay safe until the killer is definitely caught," Laura said. "I'm sorry, but it could be a number of days – but we truly believe you are his next victim, and the only way to prevent that is to keep him from getting to you."

"I understand," Clara said. "I just went to the grocery store yesterday, so I should be fine for a few days or even a week. I'll let my boss know."

"Thank you for taking this seriously," Laura said. "Again, if you do need to go out for any reason, please call me back on this number. We'll get a patrol car over to you. It's not safe for you to be outside on your own, even for a moment, right now."

"Okay," Clara said. "I'll let you know. Thanks for calling."

"Alright," Laura said, and the line went dead.

She looked up. Nate was also already off the phone; he shook his head at her.

"No answer on mine," he said.

"Mine agreed to stay inside and keep everything locked, potentially for the whole week," Laura said. "So, if his path to her is closed off, then it has to be Callie that he goes after. We haven't been able to warn her, so we need to get over there as soon as possible. It's already getting dark."

"Do you think he's going to go after her?" Princess asked. "If it's not the one we have in custody, I mean."

"I'm sure of it," Laura said, gathering her coat and everything she needed from the desk as she stood up. "He was more cautious at first, leaving a couple of days between victims. But over time, killers escalate their behavior – especially when they know that the police are closing in on them. We could expect an attack tonight. And even if he doesn't strike now, the quicker we get over there and make sure she's safe, the better."

"I'm coming with you," Princess declared.

"Hang on," Nate said. "Where are we going?"

Laura looked at him. "What do you mean?"

"The killer usually targets them when they're leaving work for the day. Do we know where she works?"

"No," Laura said. "Alright – detective, I want you to stay here with Agent Lavoie. You're going to get on Callie Scrivener's social media and find out where she works. The two of you can head over there if she would still be on shift, or if your data indicates that she would already be at home, follow me. I want to get over there as soon as possible, make sure we're covering the base we do know about."

"That makes sense," Nate nodded. "Right, Detective Tanzi – let's split the apps between us in case she doesn't have accounts on all of them."

Laura walked away to the sounds of the two of them discussing who was doing what, heading right for the precinct parking lot. The rental car keys jingled in her hand as she went.

She stepped outside into the twilight, looking up at the sky. She needed to get there now. Quicker than now.

Because as soon as it was dark enough to hide a man dressed in black within the shadows, she had this feeling in her gut.

He was going to attack – and it was going to be tonight.

***

Laura knocked loudly on the door for the second time, her hands almost feeling bruised as they met the cold plastic, and then rang the doorbell again. There was still no response. She sighed in frustration. The car was parked in the driveway. Had the killer already been here? Maybe she should call for backup, get the door broken down.

"Excuse me?"

Laura turned, whipping around in surprise, her hand going to her gun. When she saw that it was only an older woman leaning over the fence between this property and the one next door, she had to force herself to relax.

"Hello?" she said, barely even hearing her own voice over the rapid and violent beating of her heart.

"Are you looking for Miss Scrivener? I heard you knocking," she said.

"Yes," Laura replied, stepping closer. "Do you know if she's home? Her car is here."

"No, she's not here, dear," the neighbor replied. "Her sister gave birth last week so she went over there to help out. I think she took the train."

"I see," Laura said. She glanced back at the dark, silent house. "Do you know when she's going to be back?"

"I don't think she has a set plan," the neighbor said. "Possibly until they don't need her anymore."

"Right. Thanks," Laura said. She started to walk away, back towards her car, thinking.

Thank goodness for nosy neighbors, was her first thought. But behind that, there was something more. Something that worried her a lot.

If two of the interviewees from the book were out of the killer's range, then he had only two options. Either he traveled out of town and changed his MO thus far completely, going to a different city and presumably a different state, a place he didn't know well. It would be a huge risk.

And his other option was to go after the one victim he had left.

Clara Brand.

She had said she would stay inside, lock the doors, never answer them. And Laura had assured her that the killer had never broken into anyone's house so far.

But that didn't mean he wouldn't consider it if he got desperate.

Laura swore and raced to the car, grabbing her cell phone as she went. She hit dial, turned on the speaker, and threw it onto the passenger seat so she could drive as she spoke.

"Laura?" Nate's voice came through the line as it connected.

"Nate, I'm just leaving Callie Scrivener's place," Laura said, glancing over her shoulder as she moved back onto the road and started to move forward. "She's not at home. She traveled away to visit her sister this week. The killer wouldn't be able to target her."

"Right," Nate said. "Goddamnit, we just arrived at where she works. Okay. You're going to the other place?"

"Yes," Laura told him. "I'd better give her a call and let her know of the change in circumstances. Maybe we can arrange some backup as well – that patrol car is sounding like a better idea by the second."

"I'll make that call and then set off," Nate said.

"See you there," Laura replied. The call cut off, and she raced forward until she hit a stoplight. Taking advantage of the lull, she hit redial on the landline she'd called earlier – the one belonging to Clara Brand.

The dial tone rang out. The light changed and Laura surged forward, biting her lip. The tone rang again and again, filling the car.

Then it went to a generic voicemail message, and Laura swore and put her foot down further on the gas pedal.

CHAPTER TWENTY TWO

He settled in behind the armchair, letting the darkness of the shadows embrace him. It was comfortable down here. The carpet was soft enough to take away the sting of the floor, and the room was warm. He didn't mind waiting for as long as he needed to wait. Even if he eventually had to steal out away from here and find her in her bedroom, it would be fine.

It was almost a meditative experience, this part. The waiting. He'd done all the planning, all the watching, all the preparation. All that remained now was the final movement. He just had to leap up and put his ligature around her neck and pull, and it would be all over. Another one down.

This house was pretty. Nice. The carpets were soft and the armchair looked new, like the cushions would still be bouncy and supportive, everything comfortable. It was the home of a person who had everything they needed. She was still single, but did that matter? She was obviously doing well in herself. Maybe she didn't feel the need for a partner yet. She was still young.

She was young, and she was already doing better than he was.

He ducked his head, feeling the simmering rage building inside him again, trying to fight down the growl that wanted to rise inside his throat. All these people. They made him feel sick. They just went on, living their lives, being normal people. Being happy. As though none of it had even happened.

Didn't they feel the guilt? Didn't they know they weren't supposed to survive?

There was a noise on the floorboards overhead and he looked up, his senses tuned in that direction, trying to sense whether she was coming down. Seconds ticked into minutes and there was no further noise. He relaxed back into his ready posture. He would wait a bit longer.

He tasted blood and realized that in the depth of his rage, he must have bitten the inside of his lip right through. He probed the wound with his tongue. It wouldn't take long to heal. They never did. No matter how much he wanted to hurt himself, it would always heal in the end. Just like the burns on his right side. Just like the slash across his right shin where the door had cut him. Ten years, and the scars were faded to the point that he couldn't even imagine what they had looked like when they were fresh.

It wasn't right.

Ten years of trying to make up for it – of trying to find a way to get through the guilt. The memory of his mother's eyes, wide and white and seeing nothing ever again, still haunted him. It was when he'd realized that the nightmares had dropped down to once a month, not every single night, that the guilt intensified. He was forgetting her. Forgetting the sacrifice she had made for him.

That accident had taken her life, and he'd walked away with scars that he barely even noticed anymore.

How was that in any way right or fair?

And these people, they were all the same. They'd seen death and walked away from it. Their lives should have ended, but they hadn't. And what was the cost? Whether it was a car accident in which the other driver died, a school shooter who killed the others but missed their mark in one case, a bomb going off in a public place where one or two survived…

They never seemed to think about the people who hadn't been as lucky.

All of them had carried on with their lives. Brooke Ware got married and found a home, a place to raise future children. Haydn Townsend had run his store so successfully, building relationships with members of the local community, becoming such a pillar of the town that they were probably going to name a street or a building after him now. And Jessika Granger – well, Jessika Granger made him feel sickest of all. Not only had she married, not only had she made her small business a success, but she had also spent her career telling other people not to feel guilt over what they had done.

Every single day, she told people who had survived that it was okay. That they could go on living their lives. That they didn't have to feel bad.

And every day, he had lived with this guilt and this burning rage, bringing him to his knees, burning down his whole life and anything in it that might ever have brought him happiness.

All of them deserved to die for the lives they had built when they should have been dead.

There was another creak from upstairs, then the sound of footsteps quite clearly coming in his direction. He tensed, shifting his body slightly to be ready. She was coming down. She would be his soon.

As he waited, there was only one thing in his mind beyond the job he had to do. He saw her now, as he always did. He remembered the day the guilt had become too much and he had tried to take his own life.

He remembered the way she had flashed into his mind, the way he had seen her as if he was back there in the wreckage of the car, the way her white eyes had seemed to send him a message.

Don't die, son. Stay. Stay and make sure that anyone who dares to live when I did not learns the error of their ways.

She hadn't said a word, but he'd known what she wanted to tell him. Why she had appeared in front of him then.

And he wasn't going to let his mother down.

There was movement inside the room and he tensed further, his hands almost slippery inside his gloves, the ligature a reassuring presence as he wrapped it tight around his fingers for grip.

She moved through the room with light steps, and then –

The chair creaked as she settled her weight into it.

And he leapt up, the ligature ready, and looped it around her neck, pulling tight immediately, using his weight against the back of the chair to pull it so tight she had no chance of getting away.

CHAPTER TWENTY THREE

Laura knew from the emptiness of the street that she was the first to arrive. There was one car parked out front in the designated space, but she knew that had to belong to Clara. Nate, or the patrol car backup, had not yet arrived.

Laura was on her own, and she couldn't wait to take action. She had to do something. She had to move.

She got out of the car with a cautious look around, all too aware that if the killer was watching, she was turning herself into an easy target. She kept her hand on her gun as she walked with quick and quiet steps to the front door. It was totally dark now, the only light supplied by the neighboring properties or the glow from one upstairs window.

Laura reached out to knock on the door, her hand hitting it lighter than she had intended and making no sound as she faltered under the weight of a sudden headache, stunning her into pulling the punch –

Laura was inside the house, and so was Clara. She was moving through the dark, but she didn't appear nervous or even uncertain. She looked determined. Without knowing how, Laura knew this was her logic: that she would go downstairs and sit in her favorite chair without turning the lights on, and anyone who wanted to hurt her would think she was still upstairs, and she would stay safe.

She walked confidently through her own space, knowing exactly where everything was despite the darkness. She didn't need to turn on the lights. She'd placed everything here where it was. She could walk around this place with a blindfold on and one hand tied behind her back. She walked to her favorite chair and sat down, grabbing a book from the side table and a small reading light.

And the garotte went around her neck, pulling her back against the chair, the string looped into a circle and restricting her throat as her eyes flew open in shock, the light clattering to the floor.

Laura blinked. A throbbing headache launched itself through her temples so hard that she was left gasping for breath. The killer was already inside the house.

The killer was already inside.

She lifted her hand to knock again, properly this time – and then she heard it.

The clattering noise made by a light falling to the floor.

Laura knew what it was. She knew it was the killer. She didn't have time to mess around knocking and hammering on the door, shouting, trying to get him to stop because he was spooked. This killer wasn't like that. She had a feel for him now, for his determination. His usual method had been thwarted, so he had changed, adapted. He would take Clara's life no matter who tried to stop him.

She had to think, and fast.

He was in there. How had he gotten inside?

Laura rushed around the back of the property. He couldn't have known before he set off that the victim he wanted to attack was not going to be accessible.

There was a gate into the backyard which was hanging open; she pushed through it, recognizing that this must be where the killer had gone before her.

He'd probably planned to get her as she left her home, or at least as she left work earlier in the day. When Laura warned her off, she had ruined that plan. So, he must have gotten inside somehow after the fact.

Which meant that somewhere, there was a door or a window through which she could also enter.

She turned a corner –

And saw it. The back door. There was a neat hole in the glass, right next to the handle. It must have been achieved almost soundlessly with professional tools. Once he had cut the hole, he would have been able to reach inside. He could have turned a switch lock on the door handle itself, or pushed a bolt aside, or just reached for a key hanging inside the door.

Laura reached out and the handle turned when she tried it, opening the door outwards. She ran inside, the small sounds of struggle she could hear as well as her memory of the vision leading her to a room on the right-hand side of the house. She burst inside and saw them: Clara Brand in her chair, standing, dragged up to where she was leaning against the back of the chair itself and wrestling to get the ligature from around her neck. Behind her, still robed in darkness, the killer was there, his hood up to hide his face, his gloved hands pulling the ligature tight.

She reached for her gun by instinct, but the room was dark and the killer was close to his victim. Right behind her, in fact. If she shot

137

now... there was a higher than good chance that she would hit Clara, not the killer. She couldn't risk that. She couldn't take a life in the process of attempting to save it. There was only one option.

Laura ran from a standing start and launched herself across the room at the killer.

She threw herself bodily into him, knocking into him hard enough to loosen his grip. Within the rush of a moment they were both on the floor, and Clara was somewhere on the other side of the chair, gasping for breath – wheezing. Laura knew she was free but also that she wouldn't be much help, and she knew it wasn't over. The killer recovered from their knock to the floor too fast, getting to his feet and scrambling away from her – back towards Clara.

No. No, Laura couldn't allow it.

She charged at him again, this time purposely tackling him like they were playing football, aiming herself right at his middle and pushing. He stumbled back the few steps she wanted – stumbled back into the window – the locked window –

The shattering of glass filled the world around her, hundreds of tiny glittering shards exploding around them, for just a moment putting her back into the vision of the car crash she had seen from Haydn Townsend. Then she hit the ground hard, rolling over and over, the thought flashing through her mind that she was grateful Clara had cultivated grass around the side of her house instead of concrete.

But a moment of thought was all it could be. Even as she rolled she was trying to see him, where he had landed. She looked back and saw him, struggling for a minute and then falling again, and she launched herself to her feet to grab him. Before she could do anything he was up and gone, moving back toward the street.

The street – where he would be able to get away.

Laura wasn't going to allow that, either.

She charged after him. He had taken the brunt of the glass, and the brunt of the fall, too – he was heavier than her, so he had gone down harder. She had the advantage. He made it out onto the front lawn and stumbled slightly, hesitating like he wasn't sure of where to go, like he couldn't remember where he'd parked his car.

Laura didn't waste any time. She launched herself into the air again and took him down, tackling him to the ground, getting him down so she could grab his arms. She reached for her belt –

And remembered at that moment that she had used her handcuffs to restrain Sean Jardine, and never taken them back when they got to the precinct.

The hesitation on her part was enough for the killer to throw her off, making her land on the lawn again, and then he was getting into a position from where he could spring away –

Everything happened so fast then. Laura made to grab for him, but it didn't work. She was too slow. He was leaping forward, out into the street. And then the headlights swept across both of them, blinding her momentarily.

All she heard was the *crunch* of the impact.

When she was able to clear her sight enough by blinking rapidly, Laura saw the aftermath. The car had come to a screeching stop, and the doors were opening as Nate got out of one side and Princess out of the other. Their attention was on what they had hit: the killer, now laying prone on the pavement in front of them. He groaned faintly, prompting both of them to rush forward to examine him.

"Nate!" Laura called out, finding her voice weaker than she expected. He turned, saw her, and rushed over, leaving the detective with their suspect.

"Jesus, Laura, what happened here?" he asked.

"Don't mind me," she said. "Inside. He was strangling her already when I got here. In the room with the smashed window."

"It's bad!" Princess called out.

"Go," Laura told Nate, struggling her way up to her feet, finding herself more weary than badly injured. She was gradually becoming aware of small cuts from the glass, bruises from the various impacts – but nothing that would stop her from arresting a killer.

She made her way to where he lay on the street, wheezing breaths coming from his chest. His eyes were wide. His face was smeared with blood from the various cuts he'd gained going through the window. Lifting his hoodie, Laura saw a dark bruise already spreading across his midsection. It was more than possible he had internal bleeding, maybe some damage to internal organs from the hit of the car. It had been going at a good speed.

"It's over," he wheezed. He was looking at Laura. Right at her. Like he knew that, ultimately, she was the adversary who had been tracking him down, working against him this whole time. That she was the one he had to be afraid of. "Just let me die."

Laura looked right back into his eyes and pulled her cell phone out of her pocket. Thankfully, it was undamaged. She dialed and put it to her ear.

"Hello? Yes – this is Special Agent Frost. Requesting urgent ambulance assistance."

The killer groaned and closed his eyes with a half-sob, and Laura stood to wait for the red and blue lights to flash their way down the street.

CHAPTER TWENTY FOUR

"It's like the ultimate insult."

Laura looked up at Nate, bringing her a fresh cup of what could barely be called coffee from the hospital's machine. "What are you talking about?"

He sat down next to her with a grin. "Well, he was against people with near death experiences. Now we've made sure that he survived not just one, but two. He is the thing he hates... twice."

"That's true," Laura said, after a moment of thought. She glanced around at the other people in the waiting room. It was frustrating to be personally able to leave, but stuck waiting for someone else to be finished up. She'd had a bit of disinfectant dabbed on the small cuts left by the glass, and an examination to ensure there was no internal damage. She was fine, in much better shape than she had been after some other recent cases.

"Lawson West," Nate said aloud, using the name that they had discovered belonged to the killer. "He wasn't even on our radar. If it hadn't been for catching him in the act, I have no idea how we would have managed to identify him."

Laura nodded. "If he had decided to lay low until the heat was off and his victims were no longer being protected, we would have had no way to stop him."

"Sure, we would," Nate said, nudging her with his shoulder.

"What?" Laura asked, nonplussed.

"We didn't catch him because of the book," Nate said. "We would have had no idea that the book even existed if it wasn't for you. For what you *saw*." He emphasized the word enough that she would know what he meant, in case one of the others sitting in the hospital's waiting room were listening.

Laura turned that over in her mind a bit. "I guess so," she said. She hadn't really thought of it until Nate pointed it out. "I think my powers are back up to full. My, um. Deductive powers."

Nate flashed her an amused look which seemed to say *good save.* "I'm glad to hear it. Not that we weren't doing fine on the other cases

141

before, but it's good to have all the tools in our arsenal. You really knocked it out of the park on this one, Laura."

"Thanks." Laura ducked her head, surprised to find herself actually blushing. What was she, a ten year old girl? But it felt strange to have someone compliment her because of her visions. She'd never been praised for them. When she was a young girl and hadn't known that she needed to keep them secret, people had acted like she was strange or had even been afraid of her – and her parents had made it clear that it was a shameful practice she had to stop immediately.

Not that it had made any difference. The visions came whether she wanted them or not. The decision to use them for good had been the only way she could reconcile herself to the fact of having them.

"I'm really glad you told me," Nate said, his voice warm. He kept it low as he shifted in his chair, a comment just for her to hear.

"Me too," Laura said, glancing at him with an uncharacteristically shy smile.

"Agents!"

They both looked up at the word, called out by a doctor who was near the exit of the waiting room, the beginning of a hallway. They scrambled to their feet and went over to speak with him, moving aside to a small room off the main one so they could speak privately.

"I'm happy to say that both of our patients are stable," the doctor said. "Clara Brand is going to make a full recovery. She's going to have a few days or even a week or two of throat pain and redness, but it will heal completely."

"That's a relief," Laura sighed.

"It was your quick actions that did the job, so I'm told," the doctor said, peering at Laura over the top of wire-rimmed spectacles. "How are your cuts and bruises? You've been seen fully, yes?"

"Yes, thank you," Laura said, brushing it aside with a shrug. "What about West?"

"Lawson West is going to be fine as well," the doctor said. "He's got some injuries which we want to monitor for a few days, but nothing that won't heal up just fine. He might have a couple of scars from the glass cuts, and that's all. He'll need to stay as still as possible until the ribs heal, of course."

"That's fine," Nate nodded. "We can have a police presence outside his room all day and night to ensure that there's no chance of him escaping until his treatment is concluded."

Laura's phone buzzed in her pocket, and she tried to ignore it until the doctor was done. "Does he have any signs of defensive wounds?" she asked, remembering how it seemed to her that Haydn Townsend had tried to fight back.

"He has some bruising on his forearms which is a little older," the doctor nodded. "It's no scratch mark, but I gather he was fully covered in thick clothing when he carried out his attacks. Yes, I think we could make a case that the bruises were caused by one of his victims trying to get his arms away from their neck."

"Thank you," Laura nodded. The evidence was stacking up. Apart from being caught in the act by an FBI agent, there was enough against him now that she believed any lawyer in the country would advise him to plead guilty and make a full confession.

"Alright," the doctor nodded. "Take care, now."

"We will," Nate assured him, the three of them walking back out into the hall together.

"I guess we're done here," Laura said, as the doctor walked away.

"Looks like it," Nate said. "You want to go back to the motel and pack up? I'll call Rondelle."

"Excellent," Laura nodded, grinning. "You get to receive all the praise after I had him shouting at me on the phone."

"Well, you can call him if you want," Nate replied.

"Hell, no," Laura laughed. "The honor is all yours. Just in case he's not in a good mood despite our success."

She grabbed her cell phone out of her pocket as they walked back through the hospital, an eerie place right now in the middle of the night. It was quiet but somehow still busy, and even though there were areas which were completely indoors with no influence from windows, you could sense the fact that it was nighttime out there. The fluorescent lighting just seemed to be that little bit harsher, that bit more yellow.

She glanced down at the notification she'd received and nearly dropped her phone.

It was a message from Chris.

Laura paused to read it again, leaving Nate to turn around a few steps ahead, obviously realizing she was no longer keeping pace with him.

"You alright?" he asked.

Laura read the words one more time. *Will you meet me when you get back from your case?*

143

"I think so," she said, allowing herself the brave hope of a smile. "Let's get back home. I've got plans to make."

***

Laura found herself standing in that same exact spot, sweating with nerves, wiping her palm on her side before she reached out to knock on the door. One day, she thought to herself, she was going to have anxiety nightmares about this door. It seemed like every time she stood in front of it lately, something huge was happening. Something that made her want to run away. It was only the fact that she liked Chris so very much that rooted her feet in place.

When the door opened, her heart leapt into her mouth.

"Hey," Chris said, with a hesitant smile.

He was as he always was. Brown hair a tiny bit messy but with an attempt at neatness. The white button-down shirt, with the sleeves rolled up and the top button undone after a long day at work. A cup of coffee in his hand, as if he'd come right from the kitchen to answer the door and hadn't thought to put it down.

He was one of the most welcome sights Laura had ever seen.

"Hi," she said, pushing herself to walk toward and through the door rather than hesitating and making it awkward.

"Come in," Chris said, gesturing right through in the direction of the kitchen. "Please. I'll get you a coffee."

"Thanks," Laura said automatically, following him inside. It was strange. She'd been here so many times, yet now it felt odd. Like she wasn't supposed to be here. She hoped the feeling was about to go away. He wouldn't invite her over here just to tell her to never contact him again – would he?

"How was your case?" Chris asked, turning to look at her as he switched on the machine.

"Well..." Laura shrugged as she sat down on a tall stool at the kitchen island. She rolled her sleeves up to show him the myriad small cuts she'd gotten from the broken glass. "We caught the guy, at least."

"Jesus, Laura!" Chris exclaimed, rushing over. He took one of her hands and turned it to examine her arm, checking all the cuts over. The coffee was forgotten. "How does this always happen?"

"Because I'm always jumping in to save people," Laura said honestly, holding nothing back. "Because I saw a vision of the victim being choked to death and I broke in there to stop it from happening at all costs."

Chris glanced down, nodding. He hadn't let go of her hand. His thumb idly stroked across one of her fingers before he looked up and met her eyes again. "George Elwood survived," he said.

Laura's heart soared quickly. Another good deed done. "I'm really glad," she said.

"Everyone was asking how I knew that he was allergic," Chris said. "I had to pretend and tell them I just had a weird feeling."

"I'm sorry." Laura felt a genuine pang at the thought. "I didn't mean to make you lie. I know how hard that can be."

"I guess you do, at that."

There was an awkward pause. Laura didn't know what to say. Should she apologize for lying to him in the past? But surely, now, he saw that it was necessary? That she had to do it in order to protect herself – and that she had told him the truth because things were getting serious between them?

"I'm sorry I didn't believe you," Chris said. "I couldn't get my head around it. I couldn't imagine for a minute that it would actually be true. And yet, it turns out…"

"It's true," Laura nodded. "You have to understand there was no way I could have known about your patient unless I knew the way I said I did. I had no way of knowing that someone would come into your ER. It's not the kind of event you can set up in advance."

"I do understand that," Chris nodded, and she saw that he was telling the truth. "I don't… I don't think I fully understand what you can do yet, or how it's possible, but I can see that you aren't lying to me. I can see that you aren't delusional. There's something going on here, whatever it is, and I guess I need to be open-minded and listen to you about it."

Laura bit her lip. That last little bit of anxiety held her back. "You need to," she said. "Or you will?"

Chris squeezed her hand. "I will. Laura, if there's one thing this… episode has taught me, it's that I don't want to be without you. This crazy thing happened, this thing that I can't explain or understand, and you know who I wanted to talk to about it? You. I wanted to call you. Because I know that out of anyone, I can rely on you to have my back and to listen when I need to work something out. And that means something. And I have to be the same for you."

Laura nodded slowly. "Okay," she said. "Then, if you're ready, I'd like to tell you all about it – about my life, my visions, and the things they've brought me until now."

"Let me get you that coffee," Chris said, bringing the cup over – and then settling down to listen.

CHAPTER TWENTY FIVE

He sat back, running the vision through his mind again. It had been very clear: a woman who could do the same things he could, having a vision and then leaving a note on the door of her... what? Partner? The other person had to be a doctor, he could tell that much. Leaving a note like that... It was interesting. Most of the other psychics he had come across had habitually hidden their talents, even from their loved ones.

Maybe that was why it was so easy to target them. If there was any level of acceptance, if any of them ever felt they could really speak up and own their identities, then it wouldn't be so easy. They would talk among themselves, form a community. They would know. They would be aware of someone in their midst who was taking their lives.

The most interesting thing about this one was that he had seen her before. The FBI agent. He'd seen her in full uniform, windbreaker emblazoned with the logo, saving the life of a little girl. At the time, he'd thought it was better to stay away from someone like her. Someone who had both her skills and her connections wouldn't be so easy to take down.

But now...

Well, he was a lot stronger now than he had been back then. It was like every time he killed one, he absorbed something of their power into his own. Like there was a balance of the amount of power allowed to exist in the universe, and it had to go somewhere.

Not only that, but if she was talking to other people about it, then maybe she would tell her superiors. Her colleagues. And the more they talked about it, the more people learned, the higher the chance was that someone would realize and make the connection. She might even have a vision about him, and then bring down a national manhunt on his head. He couldn't let that happen.

Maybe it was better to cut her off now, before she had a chance to bloom any further. Before he got onto her radar.

He had to move fast. The closer he got to her, the worse her ability would function – but his was the same. The key, he had learned, was to get to know them and trigger the visions before you were close enough to stop them. So long as you saw them, and they didn't see you, you could learn enough about them to make them sitting ducks.

Then, quite literally – they would never see you coming.

Yes, this one would have to be his next one. He couldn't allow her to live and risk that she would stop him in his tracks. He was powerful now – but he would be more powerful still. He had a lot of growth to do. A lot of rivals still to put out of play.

Laura. That's what her partner had called her.

How many FBI agents called Laura could there be?

And now that he knew what she looked like...

Tracking her down should be easy as pie.

NOW AVAILABLE!

ALREADY COLD
(A Laura Frost FBI Suspense Thriller—Book 11)

FBI Special Agent Laura Frost's new visions make no sense: she sees victims about to die. Yet when she races to the crime scene, she discovers victims killed decades ago, and cases long closed. Is Laura losing her gift? Or is the paradox hinting at something to come?

"A masterpiece of thriller and mystery."
—Books and Movie Reviews, Roberto Mattos (re Once Gone)

ALREADY COLD (A Laura Frost FBI Suspense Thriller) is book #11 in a long-anticipated new series by #1 bestseller and USA Today bestselling author Blake Pierce, whose bestseller Once Gone (a free download) has received over 1,000 five star reviews. The Laura Frost series begins with ALREADY GONE (Book #1).

FBI Special Agent and single mom Laura Frost, 35, is haunted by her talent: a psychic ability which she refuses to face and which she keeps secret from her colleagues. While Laura gets obscured glimpses of what the killer may do next, she must decide whether to trust her confusing gift—or her investigative work.

When premonitions of killings bring her to cold cases, Laura must bridge the past and the future. Cold case after cold case makes the future no clearer. As she realizes she must crack a string of old cases to find the killer's next move, she wonders: is she already too late?

To stop the killer, Laura must enter his mind. Can she make it to the next victim in time? Or is she doomed to relive the past?

A page-turning and harrowing crime thriller featuring a brilliant and tortured FBI agent, the LAURA FROST series is a startlingly fresh mystery, rife with suspense, twists and turns, shocking revelations, and driven by a breakneck pace that will keep you flipping pages late into the night.

"An edge of your seat thriller in a new series that keeps you turning pages! ...So many twists, turns and red herrings... I can't wait to see what happens next."
—Reader review (*Her Last Wish*)

"A strong, complex story about two FBI agents trying to stop a serial killer. If you want an author to capture your attention and have you guessing, yet trying to put the pieces together, Pierce is your author!"
—Reader review (*Her Last Wish*)

"A typical Blake Pierce twisting, turning, roller coaster ride suspense thriller. Will have you turning the pages to the last sentence of the last chapter!!!"
—Reader review (*City of Prey*)

"Right from the start we have an unusual protagonist that I haven't seen done in this genre before. The action is nonstop... A very atmospheric novel that will keep you turning pages well into the wee hours."
—Reader review (*City of Prey*)

"Everything that I look for in a book... a great plot, interesting characters, and grabs your interest right away. The book moves along at a breakneck pace and stays that way until the end. Now on go I to book two!"
—Reader review (*Girl, Alone*)

"Exciting, heart pounding, edge of your seat book... a must read for mystery and suspense readers!"
—Reader review (*Girl, Alone*)

Blake Pierce

Blake Pierce is the USA Today bestselling author of the RILEY PAGE mystery series, which includes seventeen books. Blake Pierce is also the author of the MACKENZIE WHITE mystery series, comprising fourteen books; of the AVERY BLACK mystery series, comprising six books; of the KERI LOCKE mystery series, comprising five books; of the MAKING OF RILEY PAIGE mystery series, comprising six books; of the KATE WISE mystery series, comprising seven books; of the CHLOE FINE psychological suspense mystery, comprising six books; of the JESSIE HUNT psychological suspense thriller series, comprising twenty six books; of the AU PAIR psychological suspense thriller series, comprising three books; of the ZOE PRIME mystery series, comprising six books; of the ADELE SHARP mystery series, comprising sixteen books, of the EUROPEAN VOYAGE cozy mystery series, comprising six books; of the LAURA FROST FBI suspense thriller, comprising eleven books; of the ELLA DARK FBI suspense thriller, comprising fourteen books (and counting); of the A YEAR IN EUROPE cozy mystery series, comprising nine books, of the AVA GOLD mystery series, comprising six books; of the RACHEL GIFT mystery series, comprising ten books (and counting); of the VALERIE LAW mystery series, comprising nine books (and counting); of the PAIGE KING mystery series, comprising eight books (and counting); of the MAY MOORE mystery series, comprising eleven books (and counting); the CORA SHIELDS mystery series, comprising five books (and counting); of the NICKY LYONS mystery series, comprising seven books (and counting), of the CAMI LARK mystery series, comprising five books (and counting), and of the new AMBER YOUNG mystery series, comprising five books (and counting).

An avid reader and lifelong fan of the mystery and thriller genres, Blake loves to hear from you, so please feel free to visit www.blakepierceauthor.com to learn more and stay in touch.

BOOKS BY BLAKE PIERCE

AMBER YOUNG MYSTERY SERIES
ABSENT PITY (Book #1)
ABSENT REMORSE (Book #2)
ABSENT FEELING (Book #3)
ABSENT MERCY (Book #4)
ABSENT REASON (Book #5)

CAMI LARK MYSTERY SERIES
JUST ME (Book #1)
JUST OUTSIDE (Book #2)
JUST RIGHT (Book #3)
JUST FORGET (Book #4)
JUST ONCE (Book #5)

NICKY LYONS MYSTERY SERIES
ALL MINE (Book #1)
ALL HIS (Book #2)
ALL HE SEES (Book #3)
ALL ALONE (Book #4)
ALL FOR ONE (Book #5)
ALL HE TAKES (Book #6)
ALL FOR ME (Book #7)

CORA SHIELDS MYSTERY SERIES
UNDONE (Book #1)
UNWANTED (Book #2)
UNHINGED (Book #3)
UNSAID (Book #4)
UNGLUED (Book #5)

MAY MOORE SUSPENSE THRILLER
NEVER RUN (Book #1)
NEVER TELL (Book #2)
NEVER LIVE (Book #3)
NEVER HIDE (Book #4)
NEVER FORGIVE (Book #5)

NEVER AGAIN (Book #6)
NEVER LOOK BACK (Book #7)
NEVER FORGET (Book #8)
NEVER LET GO (Book #9)
NEVER PRETEND (Book #10)
NEVER HESITATE (Book #11)

PAIGE KING MYSTERY SERIES
THE GIRL HE PINED (Book #1)
THE GIRL HE CHOSE (Book #2)
THE GIRL HE TOOK (Book #3)
THE GIRL HE WISHED (Book #4)
THE GIRL HE CROWNED (Book #5)
THE GIRL HE WATCHED (Book #6)
THE GIRL HE WANTED (Book #7)
THE GIRL HE CLAIMED (Book #8)

VALERIE LAW MYSTERY SERIES
NO MERCY (Book #1)
NO PITY (Book #2)
NO FEAR (Book #3)
NO SLEEP (Book #4)
NO QUARTER (Book #5)
NO CHANCE (Book #6)
NO REFUGE (Book #7)
NO GRACE (Book #8)
NO ESCAPE (Book #9)

RACHEL GIFT MYSTERY SERIES
HER LAST WISH (Book #1)
HER LAST CHANCE (Book #2)
HER LAST HOPE (Book #3)
HER LAST FEAR (Book #4)
HER LAST CHOICE (Book #5)
HER LAST BREATH (Book #6)
HER LAST MISTAKE (Book #7)
HER LAST DESIRE (Book #8)
HER LAST REGRET (Book #9)
HER LAST HOUR (Book #10)

ALREADY LURED (Book #10)
ALREADY COLD (Book #11)

EUROPEAN VOYAGE COZY MYSTERY SERIES
MURDER (AND BAKLAVA) (Book #1)
DEATH (AND APPLE STRUDEL) (Book #2)
CRIME (AND LAGER) (Book #3)
MISFORTUNE (AND GOUDA) (Book #4)
CALAMITY (AND A DANISH) (Book #5)
MAYHEM (AND HERRING) (Book #6)

ADELE SHARP MYSTERY SERIES
LEFT TO DIE (Book #1)
LEFT TO RUN (Book #2)
LEFT TO HIDE (Book #3)
LEFT TO KILL (Book #4)
LEFT TO MURDER (Book #5)
LEFT TO ENVY (Book #6)
LEFT TO LAPSE (Book #7)
LEFT TO VANISH (Book #8)
LEFT TO HUNT (Book #9)
LEFT TO FEAR (Book #10)
LEFT TO PREY (Book #11)
LEFT TO LURE (Book #12)
LEFT TO CRAVE (Book #13)
LEFT TO LOATHE (Book #14)
LEFT TO HARM (Book #15)
LEFT TO RUIN (Book #16)

THE AU PAIR SERIES
ALMOST GONE (Book#1)
ALMOST LOST (Book #2)
ALMOST DEAD (Book #3)

ZOE PRIME MYSTERY SERIES
FACE OF DEATH (Book#1)
FACE OF MURDER (Book #2)
FACE OF FEAR (Book #3)
FACE OF MADNESS (Book #4)
FACE OF FURY (Book #5)

FACE OF DARKNESS (Book #6)

A JESSIE HUNT PSYCHOLOGICAL SUSPENSE SERIES
THE PERFECT WIFE (Book #1)
THE PERFECT BLOCK (Book #2)
THE PERFECT HOUSE (Book #3)
THE PERFECT SMILE (Book #4)
THE PERFECT LIE (Book #5)
THE PERFECT LOOK (Book #6)
THE PERFECT AFFAIR (Book #7)
THE PERFECT ALIBI (Book #8)
THE PERFECT NEIGHBOR (Book #9)
THE PERFECT DISGUISE (Book #10)
THE PERFECT SECRET (Book #11)
THE PERFECT FAÇADE (Book #12)
THE PERFECT IMPRESSION (Book #13)
THE PERFECT DECEIT (Book #14)
THE PERFECT MISTRESS (Book #15)
THE PERFECT IMAGE (Book #16)
THE PERFECT VEIL (Book #17)
THE PERFECT INDISCRETION (Book #18)
THE PERFECT RUMOR (Book #19)
THE PERFECT COUPLE (Book #20)
THE PERFECT MURDER (Book #21)
THE PERFECT HUSBAND (Book #22)
THE PERFECT SCANDAL (Book #23)
THE PERFECT MASK (Book #24)
THE PERFECT RUSE (Book #25)
THE PERFECT VENEER (Book #26)

CHLOE FINE PSYCHOLOGICAL SUSPENSE SERIES
NEXT DOOR (Book #1)
A NEIGHBOR'S LIE (Book #2)
CUL DE SAC (Book #3)
SILENT NEIGHBOR (Book #4)
HOMECOMING (Book #5)
TINTED WINDOWS (Book #6)

KATE WISE MYSTERY SERIES
IF SHE KNEW (Book #1)

IF SHE SAW (Book #2)
IF SHE RAN (Book #3)
IF SHE HID (Book #4)
IF SHE FLED (Book #5)
IF SHE FEARED (Book #6)
IF SHE HEARD (Book #7)

THE MAKING OF RILEY PAIGE SERIES
WATCHING (Book #1)
WAITING (Book #2)
LURING (Book #3)
TAKING (Book #4)
STALKING (Book #5)
KILLING (Book #6)

RILEY PAIGE MYSTERY SERIES
ONCE GONE (Book #1)
ONCE TAKEN (Book #2)
ONCE CRAVED (Book #3)
ONCE LURED (Book #4)
ONCE HUNTED (Book #5)
ONCE PINED (Book #6)
ONCE FORSAKEN (Book #7)
ONCE COLD (Book #8)
ONCE STALKED (Book #9)
ONCE LOST (Book #10)
ONCE BURIED (Book #11)
ONCE BOUND (Book #12)
ONCE TRAPPED (Book #13)
ONCE DORMANT (Book #14)
ONCE SHUNNED (Book #15)
ONCE MISSED (Book #16)
ONCE CHOSEN (Book #17)

MACKENZIE WHITE MYSTERY SERIES
BEFORE HE KILLS (Book #1)
BEFORE HE SEES (Book #2)
BEFORE HE COVETS (Book #3)
BEFORE HE TAKES (Book #4)
BEFORE HE NEEDS (Book #5)

BEFORE HE FEELS (Book #6)
BEFORE HE SINS (Book #7)
BEFORE HE HUNTS (Book #8)
BEFORE HE PREYS (Book #9)
BEFORE HE LONGS (Book #10)
BEFORE HE LAPSES (Book #11)
BEFORE HE ENVIES (Book #12)
BEFORE HE STALKS (Book #13)
BEFORE HE HARMS (Book #14)

AVERY BLACK MYSTERY SERIES
CAUSE TO KILL (Book #1)
CAUSE TO RUN (Book #2)
CAUSE TO HIDE (Book #3)
CAUSE TO FEAR (Book #4)
CAUSE TO SAVE (Book #5)
CAUSE TO DREAD (Book #6)

KERI LOCKE MYSTERY SERIES
A TRACE OF DEATH (Book #1)
A TRACE OF MURDER (Book #2)
A TRACE OF VICE (Book #3)
A TRACE OF CRIME (Book #4)
A TRACE OF HOPE (Book #5)

Made in United States
Orlando, FL
04 January 2023

28106310R00104